MASTER GUNSLINGER

By
Steve Smyrski

ISBN: 978-1-4269-4218-1 (sc)
ISBN: 978-1-4269-4219-8 (e)

*Our mission is to efficiently provide the world's finest, most comprehensive
book publishing service, enabling every author to experience success.
To find out how to publish your book, your way, and have it available
worldwide, visit us online at www.trafford.com*

Trafford rev. 10/06/2010

Trafford PUBLISHING® www.trafford.com

North America & international
toll-free: 1 888 232 4444 (USA & Canada)
phone: 250 383 6864 ♦ fax: 812 355 4082

Swallowing hard I was about to execute my plan when a voice came from behind me. I never heard anyone walk up. This was the one reason why I always liked to sit with my back to the wall.

"You killed my friend," the voice growled.

This I didn't need. My side still hurt to the point I didn't feel I could draw to my full potential. I knew I could draw as fast with my left hand but unfortunately I wasn't wearing two guns at this particular time. This left me with somewhat of a disadvantage.

"You killed my friend and now I'm gonna kill you," he announced again.

Thinking now how bad this was. I finally had the man I was searching for sitting right in front of me, with a man who now wanted to kill me to my back.

Chapter 1

A light rain was falling as the wagon traveled down the main street of Pinewood. Reining the horses was Robert Masters, a local ranch owner. Sitting beside him was his five-year-old son Vince.

Vince loved going to town with his dad because it meant getting his hands in the candy jar at the supply station. To his father Robert, it was purely business. Owning one of the largest cattle ranches in the territory, Robert was meeting with Pere Tibedeaux, the biggest cattle buyer in the Arkansas territory.

Robert pulled back on the reins to stop in front of the general store. The squealing from the hand brakes brought the wagon to a slow stop as well as the stain on the horses that were still pulling. Robert meant to have new leather applied on the brake pad but being some what of a procrastinator it would probably be a while yet.

Off to the side a man came flying through the bat wings of the saloon that was only fifty feet from where the wagon had come to a stop. The man was pushed by a much bigger man and slid to a stop on the side of his face in the dry dirt of the street.

Both men ended up out in the street away from the walk. The one man had stood up yelling, "I don't want to fight you Bart."

Right in front of Robert and his son, Bart went for his gun. The smaller man, who looked younger, flipped his gun out of his holster. Next there was an ear-shattering bang. Flame and smoke shot out of the barrel. Bart's gun never even cleared leather.

To Vince it looked like a magic trick how fast that gun appeared and fired. While his eyes were glued to the gun, Robert glanced over to see Bart fall to his knees. His hands covered his stomach trying to hold back the blood that was now staining the front of his shirt. His face was looking at the damage the bullet caused. Looking up at his assailant not able to speak a word he fell face first in the dirt.

Robert looked over to see Vince's eyes still glued to the smoking gun. This was the first gunfight Vince would witness, and he would never forget the speed at which a gun could be drawn and fired.

He didn't understand what could cause or provoke such a terrible act, but he was so affected that he was instantly determined to learn how to perfect the magic art of drawing a gun at lightening speed as he had just seen. He never noticed the death the gun had just delivered or the pain it ingested.

Vince, snapping out of his trance, jumped down and went into the store following his father. The storekeeper consoled Vince to get his mind off what he had just witnessed.

"Here boy, candy jars are here waiting for you," John announced.

"John, can you watch Vince for a bit? I have a meeting I'm already late for," asked Robert.

"Not a problem, Bob. You know I enjoy the kids when they come in," he admitted.

Vince had an older brother Cal and a younger sister Katie. Vince's errand was to get enough candy for both. Though he thought it to be free, it was actually put on Robert's tab. Vince had his bag of sweets now so his mind went back to the gunfight.

The wagon ride back to the ranch seemed shorter than usual as Vince's mind was occupied in thought. Robert tried to start a conversation with him but he was filled with too much anxiety to participate in conversation. This worried him some but figured it was an exciting time for Vince and he'd eventually lose interest in it as soon as he got home and told his brother and sister what he saw.

The next day though Vince found an old wooden carved pistol left by one of the past hired hands. He also found an old holster in the cellar. With such a tiny waist, he had to make a new hole in his belt to secure the holster and used a string to tie the holster to his skinny little leg.

Robert had no intention of his son growing up to be a gunfighter. Later when he found the wooden toy gun in Vince's bedroom, both the gun and holster were trashed, not as a punishment, but as a way to try to make sure Vince knew he disapproved of him having it. Vince was too young to know the dangers that lie in the West for young men with quick hands and fast-draw abilities. There was always someone watching and waiting to challenge you.

As Vince grew, his body took the shape of a muscular formed teenager mostly from working around the ranch. Working on a cattle ranch was not light work. Vince looked a bit older with the body he had conformed.

One day while in town getting supplies with his older brother Cal, Vince found out what street smart was all about. His father always tried to preach to him about street fights and how to avoid them, it was just that Vince was too immature to listen.

The Ballard brothers, Mike and Jake, just happened to be in the same area as Cal and Vince, and right away they wanted to claim the same territory.

Mike and Jake were brought up as bullies by the best teacher around, their father. So today would be Vince's first lesson is to what life can bring even when you're minding your own business.

Fighting was not new to Cal or Vince. Brothers' indifferences were just part of growing up. After a fist a cuff, they would pick themselves up, dust off their clothes, not talk for a few hours, and then go back to being brothers.

But Vince was going to find out real quick that a fight with strangers wasn't quite the same as tussling with your brother.

Mike and Jake started with the funning and the teasing amongst themselves getting them selves worked into a frenzy aiming the teasing toward the Masters brothers. Mike and Jake were no slouches themselves, and street fighting was not new to them. Being schooled in town and with other boys, these two bullies were hellions about to show it to the new kids.

The wagon was almost finished being loaded, and both Vince's and Cal's muscles were pumped from carrying the heavy boxes to the wagon. The sweat shine just magnified the definition of the muscles on both boys. To Mike and Jake this made a fight with these two justifiable. Cal was walking out of the store with a case of fencing nails when Mike casually walked by and stuck out his leg tripping Cal.

Crashing to the ground, Cal laid for a few seconds stunned to what had just happened. Vince, seeing and knowing instantly jumped on Mike. He was off balance, and Mike didn't go down. Grabbing Vince by his long blonde hair, he pulled him down smashing a right fist to his jaw at the same time. Vince could feel swelling immediately from the force of the punch.

Cal was getting up shaking his head clear when Jake jumped at him. Leaving the ground he landed both feet into Cal's chest, knocking the wind out of him.

Being so worn out after loading the wagon, the fight was over before it even started, making Mike and Jake look victorious.

The fight with the Masters brothers wasn't totally gone from them yet, but as they got up to defend themselves, Mike and Jake were grabbed from behind by two men wearing silver stars and everything came to an instant halt. Vince would have nothing to do with it as he delivered a final shot to Mikes face. He was determined to put a welt on Mike to match his.

"You two go on ahead," the two men ordered, "We saw what happened, and we'll take care of them."

Vince and Cal stunned from what had happened, dusted themselves off and climbed onto the wagon to head home.

"What the hell just happened?" Cal yelled at Vince.

Vince, with fire in his eyes, just sat there for a moment, then snapped, "I don't know, but it won't ever happen again." This was Vince's introduction into the society of the West and he would never forget this or be so unprepared again. Cal, the quieter one of the two, just shook his head and blew it off. Vince would not. Even though he delivered the last punch he was still mad he was hit at all.

It was eight miles back to the ranch and the quietest ride back home the boys had ever taken, both with such different thoughts. Cal would eventually let this all become history, but Vince's thinking was quite different. These two were going to pay and pay dearly for what they had just done. When they arrived home and walked into the house, those thoughts were magnified after they saw the face of their father.

"What in Sam's hell happened to you two?" Was his first response, looking over the boys torn clothes, bloodied, and swollen face of Vince.

"Get upstairs and clean up. Meet me in the study so you can explain yourselves," Robert ordered.

The explanation their father received was satisfactory and the boys were excused to head on to get ready for dinner. Later they went out and unloaded the wagon without much talk of the incident.

That night both boys bathed before going to bed. Cal laid there awhile and shortly was out snoring as usual. Vince, on the other hand, laid there playing over and over in his mind thinking of how this fight could have been different. Sleeping was not an option for this night as this young man was going to come up with some solutions before sleep ever entered his mind. After hours of contemplating, sleep overcame him and he was out. Even sleeping he had a dream of the day's occurrence except one thing in the dream was different. It was Vince and Jeb, face to face, wearing tied-down guns and staring into each other's eyes. Vince just waiting for Jeb to flinch in any way, and as he did, Vince's gun flipped out and a loud belch of flame shot out smashing a hole in the front of Mikes' chest the size of a half-dollar. Vince woke up in a great sweat, but shortly settled down with relief. He won his first gunfight, even if it was a dream.

Robert Masters had built his ranch from virtually nothing. Coming to the territory he staked and claimed the boundaries of over a thousand acres. He built a small cabin with just three rooms. Next he built a coral to hold sixty head of cattle he bought from a neighboring rancher. Knowing steers, he would deal with only the best bred cattle.

He was always considered a fair but firm man. He knew to buy when prices of cattle were down and hold out until prices were at their highest. Cattle became his first business, but slowly he started raising horses which were some of the best in the territory.

Robert's wife Karen died giving birth to their daughter Katie, and he never remarried. He buried himself into raising the three siblings the best he could with Marge Wilson, an older woman, who lost her husband years back to pneumonia. Robert and his wife Karen were like Marge's own son and daughter since she was unable to have children of her own. When Marge was forced to sell her ranch for financial reasons, Robert offered to have her move in with them in exchange for housekeeping and cooking for the family.

The ranch was expanded and the cabin was replaced with a luxurious six bedroom home. The house had four fireplaces, two back-to-back on each floor for heating with a large cast iron wood stove in a room connecting the large living room. Robert's den was also on the ground floor connecting the living room with two entrance doors.

He was presented a portrait of himself from the territory cattle association which he hung on the wall behind a large desk making it visible to the members on their frequent visits. The den also shared some blue ribbons won by Katie at various county picnics and portraits of the family. Robert never got over the loss of Karen, so his time was occupied with his business. His success came because of determination and hard work. Most of the time you would find him working along side the ranch hands and Vince and Cal.

Cal was as hard a worker as his father, but Vince was more a free bird enjoying life as it came to his liking. Young and restless, Robert knew Vince wouldn't be one to settle for ranch life.

Vince and Cal were both given their own Winchester Lever Action 44-40's to carry with them when they rode fence lines. They were taught to respect rifles and learn the safety of them, being taught that no weapon was ever to be used on a man. Shooting for food and eliminating varmints that jeopardized the live stock was what modern day weapons were acquired for.

For Cal the rifle was all he needed for he thought the same as his father about guns. Vince, on the other hand, was not satisfied with just a rifle, even though he was a sure shot with it. He would much rather have a six gun tied to his right leg. Vince had no hobbies to speak of so it was no wonder he enjoyed practicing the quick draw whenever he could. Whenever he could get to the barn after chores, he would practice drawing or pulling the gun, spinning it, and returning it to the holster. The pistol he used was acquired from one of the ranch hands that admired Vince and knew he could trust him to keep a secret from his dad. Getting faster and faster his confidence grew.

Chapter 2

I will never be threatened by anyone, anytime, or anywhere ever. I knew Cal and Dad would not approve of me with a gun tied to my side, but that will have to be accepted. I still wanted to be the fastest with a pistol, and that's just the way it was going to be.

"Vince," my father called from the doorway one afternoon. "I would like to see you in my study, now."

Darn, I knew this day would come. Knowing what it was about, I marched in to get it over with.

"Sit down Vince," Dad said while his eyes were glued to my six-shooter tied down as a gunslinger would wear it.

"Before you say anything," I started so I could get my two cents in before the lecture started. "I know how you disapprove of pistols. You taught Cal and me the dangers of wearing a gun." Then I just sat and stared.

Dad was a good listener, and would give the floor to anyone to have his say; he only asked for the same respect when it was his turn.

"I really can't give you an explanation, but I've always been fascinated with pistols as much as you are with your prize bulls," He didn't move a muscle. "Bulls can kill as well as pistols can, it's all on how a man acts and disciplines himself to prevent a problem with either." I looked into his eyes of surprisingly calmness. "I can promise you I will never use this gun for anything but interest or enjoyment. Lay your mind to rest, I will not use it on a man unless it means protecting me or my family." Quick thinking on my part. "It would be hard to protect yourself while cornered by a rattle snake if your rifle was in a scabbard ten feet away. That was a damn good example if I said so myself.

"Vince," he said in the same tone I've heard my whole life since I can remember. Settling back in his chair, he let his fingers intertwine each other across his stomach. "I've known for a long time now that you've had a pistol and have been practicing with it. I feel talking would be of no use."

I couldn't believe he was being so calm, but…that was his nature. "You go and do as you will, I brought this family up the best I could and I feel your word is good enough." He sat and thought for a few moments then continued, "Don't make me worry when you go to town." He sat up and opened the bottom drawer of his desk where he spent hours figuring, writing, and planning. He reached in and brought out the most magnificent nickel-plated .45 colt pistols, custom holster, and belt, which looked like it held twenty or twenty five shells. The belt and holsters were studded, and the leather work to die for, oops! I know those weren't the words I should use to describe it. The pistols had gold inlays to accent the nickel plating. From dad, the man I thought would take my head off when he discovered the love I had for pistols. Well, he told me, life was full of surprises, but it was also full of heartbreak and misery. "I'm holding you to your word as a Masters," he said as he handed me the gun and holster belt, "Happy Birthday," he wished.

Birthday? I plumed forgot it was my birthday and the best I could have ever dreamt of. I couldn't wait to ride out to the canyon and shoot this magnificent masterpiece.

It sure was hot this day, but chores had been completed and I was finished for the afternoon. I thought I would get an hour or so of practice this afternoon. As I walked into the house to get ready, the whole family was standing there with a cake sitting in the middle of the table with smiles on their faces. The candles were lit, and then came the birthday song.

"Oh, you guys, you didn't have to do this," I responded politely.

I felt goose bumps and my face blush. When we finished eating cake, I thanked everyone for the gifts: aftershave, two western novels, two shirts and a pair boots, which I thought would be saved for the monthly dances held at the town's community house. The rest of the afternoon, we sat around the table remembering the better things that had happened in our lives growing up. I knew how important these family things were to dad and Katie and I guess Marge also, but to Cal and me, a little was enough. Most of dad's stories included mom, which reminded us how much she meant to him, and other adventures of Cal, Katie, and me growing up.

So much for practicing with my new pistols today I thought. But that was ok, I knew how much this meant to the family, and deep down inside I hoped this closeness would always be.

I stood up, "I want to thank you all for such a nice birthday," not being much on sentimental speeches, "Thanks."

The next morning, I woke to the usual murmuring of the family downstairs. A hoot owl was just finishing outside my window, and the rooster letting out that annoying crow thing that they do as the sun rises. Today should be an easy day for me. It was my day to run the north side and check fences. I hoped to find time this afternoon to practice with my new pistols.

I could smell the bacon and coffee as I slipped my jeans, socks, and boots on. I walked over to the wash basin and splashed water on my face, ran a comb through my hair, then put my hat and shirt on.

My horse was a "Paint," all black with a white marking on his face and three white socks. He had the biggest blue eyes of all the ponies. I had Colt since born and was one of the friskiest I'd ever seen. I guess that's why he was my pick. He was a real challenge even after I broke him. He still had his time when he would let loose with the wildness in him. How he loved to run. I believe he'd run himself to death if you didn't pull back to slow him from time to time, but prick him with a spur, and he'd be off again giving all he had.

Seventeen and one day now. Breakfast was on the table smelling like a restaurant. Flapjacks, bacon, bread, and eggs were all on platters waiting to be devoured.

After breakfast, I grabbed my new pistols and belt and slung them around my waist.

Cal had both horses saddled and waiting. Today we were to ride fence line. Cal rode northwest and I northeast and agreed to meet in the middle sometime in the afternoon.

I loved riding in the morning, the air so fresh, wildlife calling, singing or whatever nature meant them to do. Rabbits sitting out from the bushes drying out letting their little bodies absorb the warm sun rays. Squirrels busy collecting nuts or chasing each other from tree to tree. It always amused me how they could jump a good 15 or 20 feet grabbing the most flimsy branches and keep going. I can't recall ever seeing one miss and fall.

The beavers were busy trying to dam the stream to their liking just to have Cal or one of the other hands break it down to keep the water flow running down to the ranch for the live stock. Deer, fox, and woodchucks trying to share the same 1000 acres as the live stock.

My job was to ride post to post, dismounting and shaking any post looking suspicious. Check the wire tension, replace any wire nails that pulled out from cattle pushing up against it, or hammer the loose ones back in.

In a matter of hours I had checked all the fences to the halfway mark Cal and I agreed on.

Now it was time to try out my new pistols, miles out of earshot. I rode down in the canyon which would help muffle the noise of gunfire. I found a log sitting and rotting away to the weather. I retrieved some cans I brought with me in my saddle bags and placed them on it. Lining them all up, checking them steady, then walked back 5 paces, 15 or 20 feet. My mind blanked out everything around me but the first can I placed on the log. The hours I had spent on learning how to draw were pure concentration, and now that movement of arm, hand and mind was just coming natural. Reflexes and accuracy are the things that needed to be continually practiced.

I could feel my hand so close to the grip, then in one smooth split second pulling the gun from the holster, thumbing the hammer back as it cleared leather, raising and pointing to the exact point to which the can sat, and pulling the trigger. Watching the can fly at the same time you hear the ear-shattering boom of the pistol let me know practice makes perfect. I was right handed so I practiced more with my left hand in order to be as fast with both.

Cans were shot all to hell, rocks were disintegrated, and I was almost out of shells. I felt real good about myself as I rarely would miss my mark. Practicing daily was helping me become faster and more accurate.

In the distance I could hear the hoofs of a horse stomping at full bore in the distance. I checked the cylinders making sure I had both fully loaded. I knew not to shoot all my ammo as you didn't know when a gun could be needed like right now. Not knowing who was riding in my direction so fast or for what reason, I was ready.

I took position behind my horse, between myself and the approaching rider. I pulled my rifle from the sheath and laid it across my saddle. I knew any second the rider would appear. My heart was pounding as heavy as ever. I took a deep breath and waited.

Suddenly I heard the approaching horse hit the skids, hooves sliding on the gravel to slow down. The approaching rider was being cautious. As rider came into view, I could see immediately it was Cal.

"What in the hell's all that shooting?" He yelled.

I could see his rifle lying across his lap ready for action too.

"Sorry Cal," I said in kind of an embarrassed voice. "I should have told you I was planning on doing some shooting today. You know how dad disapproves of it, so I practice in the valley."

"Well, you're right about dad, but you don't have to give me a heart attack worrying about my little brother," he responding with a half smirk. He knew his little brother could hold his own in a tousle.

The afternoon was cloudy with the sun popping in and out wherever there was a break in the clouds. There was a cool breeze which kept the riding pleasant.

"Let's ride the fence to where we were to meet and head home. I didn't see any breaks in the wire or poles but quite a few loose nails," he suggested.

It was all small talk on our ride home, but it didn't bother me as I was enjoying looking at the hills and clouds. My mind was going a mile a minute. I was already looking forward to my next practice.

As we pulled up to the stable, Dad was standing there as if he was waiting for us.

"Hey pop," Cal said in a soft voice.

When he didn't answer right away, I asked, "What's wrong?"

"I hope nothing," he replied. "Katie rode to town earlier to have her bridle repaired and pick up a few things at the General. She should be back by now. It's going to be getting dark soon. I'm a little worried."

Robert Masters, a man with something always going on business wise, but one thing he usually was not, was a worrier. Katie had been to town many times. Today it was as if he knew something was wrong.

Cal and I looked at each other when Cal said, "I'll go."

Dad smiled a thank you. He brightened up some, "Thanks Cal, we'll keep dinner warm for ya."

"I'll hay down the stalls and fetch fresh water for the horses," I offered.

"That's a fair trade," Cal said in a low voice as he wheeled his horse around and galloped down toward town. Soon the sound of hooves hitting the trail vanished and all was quiet.

Cal hadn't gone but about four miles when he saw a wagon sitting in the middle of the trail. He had a slight panic attack when he didn't see anyone around. His heart started to go normal again when he saw Katie stand-up.

"Hey sis, what seems to be the problem?" he asked.

As he got closer, he could see she was stooping to look at the right rear wheel that was about to come off.

"I don't know, everything seemed fine going into town, but coming home I started to feel a wobble. Thank goodness I looked back when I did." she answered.

Getting off his horse, he checked the wheel with some suspicion, since the wagon was recently serviced having all the wheels greased and checked.

Cal's inspection told him that the pin was gone, and that shouldn't be. "I think someone has fooled with this. Did you notice anyone near the wagon at all in town?"

"No, but then I wasn't looking," she said concerned, "I had no reason to."

"Oh well little sis, I'll go find a branch and stick it where the pin was, that should get us home. Dad's worried, so we best get home as darkness is closing fast," Cal announced.

Chapter 3

It was going on about four hours. Dinner was cold with no sign of Cal or Katie and it was dark. Both dad and I thought they should have been back by now.

I had been playing with Chester, our dog, by the fireplace. The name was given to the dog by Katie after one of dad's best cow hands left. Chester Lang had been with dad for years but all of a sudden he got this urge to move on and look for his destiny. Katie really liked Chester and cried often after he left. So when this stray dog showed up at the ranch one day, all skin and bones, Katie took him in and nursed him back to health.

"Chester, that's what I'm gonna name him," she laughed.

Chester had grown to about 90 pounds with a fine shiny coat of brown hair, and a strong chest showing muscles throughout his body. Not much of a cattle dog, he spent more time scattering the cattle than herding them. It was all fun and games to him and to tussle with him on the ground was like tackling a lion. He loved the outdoors but we kept him in at night to be sure he would not stampede the herd or come home with skunk smell, or worse yet, if that was possible, come in with porcupine needles stuck throughout his nose.

All these things had happened before. It took Cal and me over an hour getting those darn needles out of old Chester one time. The needles of a porcupine are barbed and don't pull out if in too deep. They would need to be pushed through to get them out. The ones that break off are the tough ones. For days they would hurt ol' Chester until they would fester and come out by themselves tormenting the heck out of the poor dog.

Dad was worried as all get out and remarked, "They should have been back by now, Vince."

I knew what he was hinting at and knew there was only one thing to do.

"I'll ride out and see what's keeping them," I volunteered, figuring I'd run into them by the time I got my horse saddled. "Come on Chester, let's go get Katie."

I didn't have to say that twice. He almost took me off my feet as he flew by to get out the door. It wasn't completely dark as the moon shone full. You couldn't make out particulars of any one thing but everything was recognizable. Chester stood there panting with anticipation as I saddled Colt, which took a few minutes as being so frisky made it hard sometimes.

Tonight I was in no mood for fooling around. It was late and I was full from eating too much. I was ready to sit in front of the fireplace have a game of checkers with dad before turning in. Marge was already getting out her supplies to knit for the evening.

Colt gave his one or two teasing kicks then settled in for the trip toward town. I slid the Winchester in the sheath and swung the pistols around my waist. I didn't check the ammo since I didn't expect any trouble. Trouble was scarce in the area and had been for some time.

Colt showed no reason for caution as Chester just ran along as we made our way. The moon and stars were shinning as if in some type of paradise. Crickets and frogs sang their peace offerings as we rode and a hoot of an owl, which I never really understood, because I never saw or heard but one at any given time so I always wondered who was he hooting to.

Riding over a rise that rounded the trail, I saw the outline of Katie's wagon with two horse silhouettes. But no sign of Cal or Katie till we were about 20 yards off, that's when I got a real sick feeling in my stomach. I saw both on the ground. Something was real wrong. Cal was sitting against the wheel of the wagon to his back. I yelled to them, but there was no answer.

The next thing I did was pull my gun while approaching the wagon. I gave a fast cautious look around, and then jumped down. Katie was lying face down with blood covering the back of her dress. Cal was sitting up against the wagon wheel. It looked like he had been shot twice in the chest, Dead!

I immediately went to Katie to find she had been stabbed. Her clothes were torn and the ground around showed she struggled for her life.

Time stood still, none of this was sinking in. I knelt at Katie's side seeming like time stood still. I pivoted my body to Cal. His eyes still open just starring. He wasn't seeing anything, he was dead for sure. Finding the strength I ran my hands over his eyes to let him sleep.

I remembered kneeling there dumbfounded, starring in such disbelief, my mind was blank. This could not be as it seemed. This couldn't even be a dream because I never had one this bad. Chester was licking Katie's face as to coax her to wake up, I pushed him away. I noticed whoever did this was scratched up pretty good as her finger nails were filled with flesh.

I stood-up panning the area for anything, any kind of explanation. Finding none, I looked at the wagon sitting lopsided. The wheel laying on the ground and the end of the axle buried an inch or two from the weight of the wagon.

I saw Cal with two bullet wounds had dragged himself from Katie's body to prop himself against the wheel. I saw no way he could have managed the strength to do this.

"Shake if off," talking to myself. "Do something, don't just stand there."

There were no tears in my eyes, I was so sick I couldn't see or think straight. I wanted a reason, someone to be here with me so I could understand.

Nothing had been taken that I could see. This was so senseless, "Why? Why?" I found myself yelling, but no one to hear.

I faintly remember picking up Katie and laying her tiny lifeless body in the wagon, putting my handkerchief behind her head. Then laying Cal next to her and covering their bodies with his saddle blanket.

I struggled to get the wheel back on the wagon, securing it with my knife where the pin was missing.

I tied both horses to the wagon and walked watching the knife making sure it did its job holding the wheel on. We had four miles to go. I knew this was going to be a long four miles. Chester never left my side walking next to me looking up at me for attention. I could give him none.

"What is this? What just happened?" Thinking as I walked in a trance.

Good thing the horses knew the way back to the ranch. My tears were so thick everything was a blur.

I tried to get it together. I wish I had come earlier. Could Cal have told me what had happened. Now he was dead,

I knew nothing. Chester walking along side of me as if he knew what a tragedy we just came upon.

We were at the entrance of the ranch when I pulled my colt and fired it over and over wanting dad to come running out and help me, reason with me, tell me it would be all right, anything.

No one came. Nobody could have slept through the shots of a .45. I dropped the reins and went to the door. Pushing the latch of the double doors, I almost tripped over Dad who was lying on the floor. He had been shot to death.

I yelled for Marge, but got no response. What was happening? Where were the hands? Ahh, Friday was payday. They would have gone into town like any other Friday night. I bent down to see if Dad was breathing. I went to the living room where I found Marge. Sitting in her favorite chair where she had been knitting, or crocheting, or whatever you called it still in her lap. Her front covered in blood, shot just like Dad.

What's going on and for what reason? When Mom died, Cal and I were sent outside to play and when we were called in, we had dad to comfort us. As we grew older, Marge was there to explain life's way and God's work. As we grew, we learned a lot of life and of God's ways, that's what helped us grow and understand. That was Marge's philosophy. But now I was standing here alone. What was I supposed to learn? What was I supposed to understand?

As I stood there, I looked around the room. There was no sign of forced entry and there was nothing misplaced. No signs of trouble or a struggle. This was just too much for one person to take. I wanted to sit down, close my eyes, and open them to find everything all right. Marge would call us to the table, and we would all sit down as a family and talk and laugh, drop a scrap or two for Chester, and get a scolding for doing it.

Now everything was dead silent. Chester went over to lie at Marge's feet. I guess that's what the meaning of shock is, because I was experiencing it.

Then it occurred to me to walk to Dad's office and look. There was my answer. The room was in shambles. Dad always had quite a bit of cash on hand which he kept in his top right desk drawer. The cash was held down by the weight of a .45, but now the draw was empty, gun and money missing. There were papers thrown all over the place. What else was someone looking for. The safe was still in place and appeared to be untouched, but that would always be the case because I believe it was a better unit than the one the national bank had. Without dynamite, it wasn't going to budge. Even then it was doubtful.

The three of us were always told that the safe held our futures, our inheritance. We just took it with a grain of salt knowing Dad would be with us forever, and he had plenty of time to tell us what that all meant. Now he was gone. They were all gone.

It was late, 3:00 a.m. I heard the chime of the mantle clock. I think that was what snapped me out of whatever trance I was in. I ran out and rode for town as fast as Colt could get me there. I had to find the sheriff; I had to find the hands, Ben and John. If I couldn't intercept them before they got home, what would they do? What would they think?

Dad had raised us as normal boys, not too much on the lay of the land. Yeah, we knew cattle, horses, and how to buy and sell, how to run a ranch, and how to be a boss when Dad was off on business. But no one ever told us what to do if the whole family was to expire.

I taught myself how to use a gun. Could things have been different if Cal also learned. What did he face out there with my sister? Would it have made a difference? Was he face-to-face with a man where quickness could have saved him and Katie or were they bushwhacked with no time for defense?

My mind was going now. When I got to the spot where I found Katie and Cal, I pulled back on the reins, dismounted and gave a quick look around knowing this could be the last chance before the ranch hands rode by messing up any clues.

The moon was still shining bright as I started looking. For what, I didn't know. Anything, anything at all. I had no idea what I was looking for; I just knew I had to look. There were boot prints, Cal's, mine, and someone else's but whose were whose? They seemed to be the same size; the packed dirt didn't help me. If I could get the Sheriff out here before anyone else traveled by, there might be a chance to find something I missed.

I was ready to mount Colt when my eye caught something unusual. One of the shoes of one of the horses had a break in it, and I saw the print marked over and over, meaning that the horse with a broken shoe had to be the one of the killer. It wasn't Cal's, which I was positive of and it wasn't Katie's wagon puller, which I also doubted. Finally, I stumbled onto something. Also, one of the shoes had a nail missing as you could see from the raise in the dirt, which is caused when the shoe is pressed into the soil and the soil fills into the hole where the nail was. But it wasn't the same shoe as the one that was broken.

One thing Cal and I were brought up to do was care for the horses' hooves. I was sure I found three excellent clues that would stay in my head. That was all I could see in the light the moon graced me with. I looked for some spent shells, but the killer thought enough to grab them up before he left. It also showed signs of just four horses; Cal's, Katie's, mine, and the person's horse of which I was going to hunt down at any cost.

I jumped back on Colt and bolted for town. I hoped to get the Sheriff back to the scene before anything was disturbed.

When I pulled into town, the only life was in the saloon. It was so late even the piano playing had stopped. I heard voices of a bunch of drunk cow hands and ladies who were after their money.

There was a faint light at the Sheriff's office. As I pulled up, I had to pull back on the reins at full strength to keep Colt from going straight through the front door. It was enough ruckus to see the oil lamp brighten, and the front door fling open. The Sheriff was rubbing his eyes fighting to focus. Tonight wasn't a night I would know what that felt like. My adrenaline was at such a high, I was ready wide awake.

Sheriff Ketchum was a personal friend of Dad's and knew the whole family. "Whoa boy, what in tar nation is going on," he was more awake now, "I thought we was about to have a horse inside for coffee."

I explained as steady and as clear as I could of what just happened.

"Hang on, let me get my hat!" he yelled as he ran back in the office.

In a flash he was on his horse yelling to me, "Lead the way."

I told Sheriff Ketchum everything I found, which he saw for himself on arrival at the scene, plus a few of his own which he kept to himself. Same back at the ranch.

"Nothing more we can do for right now. Come, I'll ride with you, and we'll bring the bodies back to town," he offered with sympathy.

Chapter 4

As days went by, I felt something change in me. I was alone. I had some kin, but they had settled out in California so Ben and John were my family for now. Ben had been the foreman for my Dad for four years, and John had been on payroll for about three. All other help during drives were temporary. Mostly drifters or men picked by Ben himself.

Ben had a good perception of people. He hired only men who he felt he could trust. That went for the gunmen hired for transporting money from the cattle drives also.

Ben tried to hire the best men he knew. I rode on many of these deliveries and always felt comfortable with the men.

Money, power, and greed have the possibility of turning the best men bad so I kept a part of suspicion in my mind on all men. Something my dad brought me up to believe. Now my mind was aching from thinking of anyone I had been in the presence of that could have done such an inexcusable thing. Especially Katie, who never saw the bad in anyone.

The things I saw that night repeated themselves in my brain. If I wasn't thinking of Something else or staying occupied, I relived that night over and over. My dreams were a continued reoccurrence of the same thing. What had they experienced I only prayed they had a quick death.

The person was going to pay for this and pay dearly. This was me, Vince Masters, promising myself. No matter what it takes or how far I have to travel, I will find the hombre that did this.

I left the ranch in the hands of my father's lawyer, Mr. Bronson and Ben to keep the business going until I could return.

All monies from the cattle and my Dad's savings would be held in an account in the National Bank. I wouldn't need a lot of money for where I was heading.

The first week I spent my time in town, watching and listening for any clues. My eyes glued to any hoof marks around the livery, saloons, or Queen's Stay Hotel. I asked at the livery stable if anyone was in that would have had a shoe repaired. I sat in at card games keeping my ears open for any information.

People in town were always good to me, knowing the family and me, but now two Colt pistols were a part of Vince Masters and it was to be known they were to be used in the execution of the party connected with my family's death.

Sheriff Ketchum and I both agreed whoever the guilty party was had known my family, worked at the ranch one time or another, or at least connected in some way.

I had no idea how much cash my father kept in the drawer, but it was usually a lot so he could get to it without bothering with the safe. Even though this person couldn't open the safe, he still got a substantial amount for the chances he took. I hoped he thought it was enough because whatever the amount, he'd pay for it with his life.

"Enjoy it while you can," I'd repeat in my mind.

The sheriff warned me to be careful and not take the law into my own hands. He also had told me of a suspicious person who left town earlier. He promised to help as much as he could, but if the killer had skipped town, I was more or less on my own. He would contact the territorial marshal and put him on alert.

Bounty hunters were no help to hire unless they were given a name or poster to work from. I could pay them dearly but knew not to expect much without names or descriptions.

Finding that my Mr. Bronson had access to Dad's safe in case of his death, I transferred the contents and money to the National Bank, which I'd have to admit, was enough to take care of us for years after it was distributed. But now I'd burn it all to have my family back.

A week had gone by with no trace to follow-up on what evidence I had been found.

If the killer had his horse's shoe fixed and that nail replaced, there would be no more clues to help me.

I knew Ketchum would do what he could, but his job didn't stop just to help me find a killer. Killings in town had not been a problem except for an occasional gunfight, which would involve two drunks in a card game or over a woman.

But a massacre of a whole family never happened that I knew of.

I felt lonely. I knew the Sheriff and locals, but what could they do for me.

There was only one thing on my mind; to find and take care of this killer. My life in such mayhem, I was not thinking straight. I wanted revenge each day, week, month or year if that's what it took. I was on a mission.

There was so much against me. I was brought up on a ranch, and even though I drove cattle, it was local. Never was I out of the state or even distant territory. Dad always kept Cal and me around the ranch as much as possible.

I'm sure now, if he was alive, he would have agreed that it was a mistake.

It was time for me to head west where the only clues I had, pointed.

I harnessed the wagon and tied Colt to the back. The last stop was the General Store for supplies I would need to keep me going for a few days.

Chapter 5

While I was in the store, I met a man, Jeb Currie. He had heard from talk around that my intentions were to head out after the killer. He introduced himself and explained he was headed west to meet up with his two brothers and would be glad to accompany me for a bit.

He looked physically fit. It wasn't hard to tell as it looked like his muscles were trying to tear out from the clothes he wore. The way his six gun was worn I figured he could use that as well. I was skeptical as I knew nothing about this man, but I would take the chance since I really didn't want to be alone. Maybe this man could help me in my search. Dad always said two heads were better than one.

Jeb's idea was the same as mine and Ketchums. Whoever was responsible for what had happened wasn't likely to stay around or near here. He would run for a new territory. What I couldn't understand is why not just rob a bank. I knew he got quite a sum of money from the desk, but that would mean he would have known my Dad, my family, and even be familiar with the outlay of the ranch. He would know the right time to come to rob. Maybe killing wasn't on his mind, just robbery or was it the killing he intended, and the robbery just a bonus?

I had such headaches just from my mind going over and over what the possibilities were. For such a tenderfoot, I would quickly learn the way of the West, thinking it smart to have someone to travel with and teach me as time went on.

Jeb and I rode past three or more towns because that's what they were - small towns. Knowing a killer would not be able to blend in with a small town, we would continue for the larger, more populated towns. The first few nights we bedded down under the stars. We didn't have to deal with people or the hassle of checking in and out of hotels or livery's.

It gave me the chance to get to know Jeb as I was still stand offish of this stranger. The more we talked, the more I knew he was a man I could trust. We had so much in common. He talked of his childhood, growing up with two older brothers, working a ranch till his dad had a chance to buy a general store from a widow in town. He and the three helped run the store while keeping the cattle ranch going.

As time went on, his brothers knew there was more to life and headed west. He stayed behind because of guilt as well as being too young. Three years of trying to maintain the ranch, he finally asked his dad to sell out so he could head west also. He was now older and heard his brothers were doing well. West was the place to go.

Through the years he learned to ranch, finished his schooling, and learned to handle a gun. "Did you ever shoot a man?" he asked one evening.

I took a long pause and swallowed hard. What was this leading to? Did I misjudge this man? It's been a week we've been traveling together, growing to trust each other, and now a question like this?

"No," I said. That's all I could get out.

"Well I have," there was solemnest in his voice. "One late afternoon when my dad was closing the store, a man walked in to rob him. I was in the back cleaning when I heard, "Get the money and get it fast!" he continued. "I came out from the back seeing a man backhand my dad. I had just put my gun on since we were closing, and that was the misfortune for this man. He didn't see me come out. Preoccupied with my dad and wanting money, he didn't even notice me. When he turned his head his jaw dropped. He was holding a gun but by the time he could turn it, mine was out and feeding him lead."

I had admiration for Jeb. I was wishing I had the chance to come on the scene to protect my family as he did.

"When I saw this man drop his gun and clutch his chest, there was no remorse in me." I starred into his eyes and said, "Die you bastard, die." "Could I do it again? You bet I could."

"So you're pretty fast with that gun?" I asked.

"Uh huh, I was that day. I didn't even remember pulling it," he looked down at the camp fire, "I just remember watching his chest turn wet red and him falling to his knees looking dead into my eyes, like it wasn't supposed to go down like that."

The rest of the night was pretty quiet. We turned in early for a good night's sleep so we could get an early start in the morning. The sky was clear lit with the help of the stars and a full moon. There was a slight breeze which offered us a comfortable night's sleep. In the distance a lone wolf could be heard as was owls and other night predators.

I woke up to the smell of coffee and the sizzling sound of bacon. I don't know what it is, but to me the best smell of any meal is the aroma of coffee and the distinct smell of bacon. Jeb was sitting on a chunk of log sipping on his second mug of coffee already.

"Sounded like you slept good," Jeb snickered. "You snored the whole night."

Cleaning camp we were back on the trail. We weren't a mile or so when off in the distance, Jeb caught the sight of a dust trail. A rider was riding to all get out.

"Have you ever seen an express rider before?" Jeb asked. "Well now you have," responding without waiting for an answer.

"How can you tell?" I asked inquisitively.

"He's riding light and you can see the mail pouches tied to the back of his saddle."

While riding, we observed changes. All along the trail we had observed poles spaced at a distance where wire would eventually be strung along the top. This was the beginning of the telegraph which was already eliminating the express rider in many areas.

The next town we came to we figured we would stop. I wanted to do a little investigating as well as picking up supplies. It was larger than I first noticed as we rode in. It had a couple of saloons and a larger hotel than most. Our first stop was the livery. We threw a couple of dollars to the keeper to take care of the horses and treat them with a little oats. He must not have been tipped very often as he enthusiastically took the horses and started to spoil them to tender handling.

While I started questioning the keeper, Jeb went onto the saloon for a beer.

"Looking for a rider, friend." I asked with hope.

"Everyone seems to be looking for someone stranger," he answered.

"This fella would have needed a broken shoe replaced," I said while glancing around the stable.

"I did just a few days ago replace a broken shoe, but there's not much I can tell you as there was a stage team I tended to also. But I believe the shoe I replaced was on a horse not belonging to the team," he remembered.

"Can you recollect anything about the fella riding or what the horse looked like? Anything at all, friend?" I pleaded.

While he stood there rubbing his whiskers, looking into space, I immediately knew his game, so I flipped him a dollar. You'd be surprised how a dollar can jog a mans memory.

"Well, I recollect there was nothing special about the horse or gear, just a plain brown mare I believe. The rider was a strange dude, like his mind was just on getting the shoe replaced and get back on the trail."

"Did you notice a brand?" I asked in a sound of hope.

"I'm sure I did, but not to have remembered it."

"Can you describe this dude in any way?" I pleaded.

"Well he was a big man, looked like he'd been riding long and hard. Wasn't the friendliest fella I ever met either. He went on to the Bears Den Saloon while I tended to his horse."

"Thanks friend." I said as I turned, "Be back in a while. Just take good care of these ponies, they're plummed tired." I said bearing him a crack of a smile.

"Sure will, mister." he promised. "You might want to watch your self mister. The Bears Den is a pretty dangerous place for a stranger looking for someone. They may be looked at as the law and that wouldn't be healthy."

The Bears Den was the smaller of the saloons in town. Wondering where the name came from, I walked through the swinging doors and glanced around. I didn't know if it was the bears head mounted above the bar or the grizzly looking patrons hanging around the bar and tables. The girls looked like rejects from a more high class established place.

It didn't take long to find Jeb. He was up against the bar trying to drink a beer with one hand while fending an angry call girl with the other. She took the hint and left by the time I stepped up. I looked and said, "Just missed your chance, Jebbie." and chuckled.

"Funny." he said. "I looked into the Pearl Handle, but I was a little too dusty to take the chance. It's pretty classy."

"Yeh, I guess we fit in a little better here, huh?" He asked.

"Beers beer," he said with a smile and then chugged the rest of his glass setting it down. "Come on, let me buy you one, Vince," as he snapped to the bartender for two beers.

There was a hum of the patrons talking but not loud enough to pick up on any one conversation. Two tables were occupied with card playing. Others were some big bruisers in some heavy conversation, probably local prospectors. The piano sat vacant so there was nothing to drown out the voices throughout.

Jeb finally motioned to a table and we sat enjoying a couple more beers. I was actually fine standing after the time we'd spent in the wagon, but the chairs were half comfortable and the beer was actually better tasting than I would have figured in a place like this.

Jeb told me a few stories of his past and I mostly listened. Half listening to what he was saying and half thinking of the supplies we needed to pick up while in town.

"Let's get pal, we got some supplies to get and get outta here. I'd like to put a few miles behind us before dark, but not till I speak to the bartender."

Chapter 6

Now they say timing is everything. We weren't looking for trouble and sure didn't need any. Off to our left, we heard a loud voice with authority, shout, "Just lift and drop those side arms down to the ground!"

It was the town marshal facing two ornery looking fellas. We had no idea what this was about nor did we want to. Both men were looking all business and trouble with their guns hanging and tied low ready for business.

I gave the surroundings a quick glance and saw a third man off to the side. The marshal didn't pick up on him.

"Watch that fella there, nodding to Jeb."

Seeing the other two weren't going drop their guns and the marshal was out gunned, I slowly walked up along side him. I think he was about to tell me to step out of the way when I said under my breath, "There's more than these two. I'll take the one on the left." I was standing on his left side.

"Put your guns down, I'm not gonna tell ya again!" he warned.

The two hombres now gave me a quick stare. I thought they were going to concede. They must have thought their friend was going be their ace in the hole. They tensed up with meanness showing they were ready to go for their guns. All of a sudden there was an explosion to the side of me. Their friend had drawn and Jeb had shot him. That shot triggered the others to drop down for their guns. I pulled my Colt and fanned two quick shots, one in each of them. A split second later I heard the marshal's gun bark. He would have been outdrawn and dead. I watched the two fall to their knees. Blood was staining the front of their shirts, one falling face first to the floor, the other to his side. I glanced over to see their friend hanging on to the hand railing, holding his side. His gun was lying in saw dust. Blood was already streaming into his boots.

"Darn, was that fast!" the marshal said, staring at me wondering who I was and where I came from.

Jeb walked over and said, "You better take care of that one Marshal, he was gonna take you out for his two friends there. They weren't even gonna have to draw."

By now there was quite a crowd. The marshal pointed to two men and said, "Get him to the jail and fetch the doctor, you men," pointing to a few more who he obliviously knew, "Get those two down to Sam." Sam was the livery stable keeper, also the town's undertaker. "Follow me," watching Jeb and I.

I didn't feel Jeb and I needed to stay around and make ourselves known. I wanted to get the supplies and get down the road. I just killed not my first man, but two, and my stomach didn't feel right.

"Marshal," Jeb asked, "if we can, we'd like to pick up the supplies we came to town for and get about our business" he quickly added, "I think you know what just happened and you're alive to be the sheriff for another day. Just recognize us as two concerned citizens that just happened to show in the time of need."

That was some smooth talking. It worked too.

"Go then partners and thanks, maybe there's something I wouldn't want to find out about you two anyway, the way you handled those guns," the sheriff answered.

"No Marshal," Jeb added, "just wanted to keep things fair, we're on the law side."

We got to the General Store, filled the list we made up and headed for the wagon.

"Which way did this stranger go?" I asked Sam, "The one you fixed the broken shoe for?"

"I pity this man if you're after him for any other reason than holding church service friend," he said, pointing in the direction the rider left. "The way you handle a gun I'd hate to be the one that crossed you."

Neither of us said anything. We jumped up on the wagon and we were out of there. Colt was doing a little bucking until he could get in step with the speed of the wagon.

Down the trail some, Jeb's first comment was, "Well how do you feel now that you've killed two men?"

"I don't rightly know," I retorted, "they got what they bargained for by trying it in a cheating way."

"Where did you learn to throw down a gun like that yet not kill a man? Have you told me everything there is to tell? Honestly?" he insisted.

"Yes Jeb, honestly." I looked over at him, he saw in my face I had never shot a man before. "As for my draw, I didn't know how it would hold up to a gunfighter, but it's the result of years of practice."

"You know that town would be without a marshal had we not been there right?" Jeb asked.

"That's the only reason I got involved. If it were just the two idiot cattlemen, I would have been a spectator and watched," I confessed.

"Maybe it's a good thing things worked out the way they did then."

"Why do you think he let us go without drilling us for our names, the marshal I mean?"

Jeb shrugged his shoulders, "I think he knew he was lucky to still be breathing and not lying filled with lead waiting to be buried."

I smiled over at him. "And that smooth talking had to have helped too, huh?"

"Uh huh."

It was time to start looking for a place to hold up for the night. With what had just happened, setting camp off the trail and into the woods, it would make me feel better. My mind was still on what happened and had to deal with that in my own way.

I went off collecting fire wood after finding a place for camp. Jeb did the cooking. This turned out to be quite a day for two riders learning about each other. I knew we had a common trust for each other, and both knew our backs could be watched and protected.

As we retired for the night, I laid there remembering what I had witnessed when I was such a small boy. Up until today, I was amazed with the quick draw, but it never really sunk in my brain as a kid what it meant to be shot. Now my mind was reliving the holes I saw in those two men's bodies, realizing how real death is. There's no coming back.

Sure I shot up tin cans and rocks, but today I was up against a man who could shoot back. What if they had been quicker than me. I never had any way of gauging how fast I was. In my head, I knew I was fast and today, thanks to the good Lord, I was fast enough. But what about the next time a similar situation came up?

I rolled to my side. Jeb was lying there also. "Can't sleep?" I asked in a low voice.

"No, just thinking of what happened back in town." He gave a slight yawn. "Sure glad it wasn't me that went up against you Vince. I didn't even see that gun come out, just the blaze jump from the barrel. It sounded like one shot, but I knew two. Then I heard the marshal's gun go off. He would have been dead Vince."

"Well there could have been maybe two of us dead had you not taken out that other hombre," I confessed.

The night was quiet; lying there watching the sky showing promise of rain as the bright stars were giving way to cloud cover. The faint sight of thunder and far away lightening confirmed what was ahead. Still we heard a lone coyote howling out to the sky and the hoot of an owl every 15 or 20 seconds.

The next morning we woke to a slight drizzle, but not heavy enough to prevent getting a small fire going for breakfast and coffee. Finishing breakfast, wiping up the pan with the last of the briskets we had made, Jeb poured one more cup of coffee for the both of us.

Dowsing the fire and packing the wagon with our gear, we were ready to continue our way to the next town. The trail was in pretty bad shape so we both stayed alert watch the wheels as they fought to stay together with each pot hole they hit.

The drizzle was getting heavier now turning to rain. Pulling up our collars, we let the brim of our hats do the work of keeping the rain from going down our backs. I took notice of how the weather was changing each day. Winter was coming and each day was warning us to prepare for such.

Once back on the trail, I started wondering how I was ever going to find this killer. From the information, what little that was, we were headed in the right direction. Already I was looking for the next town with anticipation of finding what I was after. There were many stage depots since the towns were spread miles apart. Many of these towns were just being established. Populations of 20 people or less had no law, and a saloon which acted as the general store, a doctor's office with no leader to speak of. These people lived on hope and prayers of growing, bringing more settlers to make stakes. No matter how small, there was always a general store to pick up needed supplies. If a stranger was to come to such a small town, he would be remembered.

A man heading west must have someplace special on his mind, not usually a small town unless there was plenty of mining with promise. If a man was scared of the law or any one following him, he would head for Mexico. I figured this killer thought he was scott free and was headed west to settle with what money he had. That what I was betting on and hoped I was right.

Jeb and I followed the route of the stage. Stage coaches went to and from larger towns or settlements. Anyone needing to go to the smaller town would have to hire a horse or horse and wagon to make the connection.

I've come accustom to having Jeb around. He was showing me the way of the West while teaching me direction. But I knew I was going lose him when he located his family. I kept thinking how great it would be to reach the completion of my search with him by my side. He was a real honest man and proving to be a loyal friend.

The rain had slowed to a drizzle, but the cloud coverage was keeping the temperature down making travel somewhat uncomfortable. Breaking out the coats was the answer to stay comfortable as we traveled on.

It didn't take long for the trail to dry out. The ground was so dry it sucked up all the water in no time. Dust was already puffing up as the hooves of the horses stepped.

"We might think of greasing those wheels and checking the axles at the next town we come to. Dealing with a broke axle out on the range wouldn't be my idea of easy traveling."

Chapter 7

It was mid afternoon as we came over a rise in the trail. Jeb had been riding his horse.

All of a sudden I saw it rear straight up and twist without any warning. Jeb had no chance to prepare for what was happening and was headed off the back as if he'd been shot.

"Snake!" Jeb yelled, as he landed on the ground with a thud.

I didn't take me long to take notice of the danger or understand Jeb's desperate yell. I had my gun drawn shooting one of the biggest rattlers I'd seen since back home at the ranch. I missed the head but the bullet cut the snake apart about six inches back of it.

Jeb layed still for a few moments until he realized the snake was no more of a threat. Then in a shaky voice, admitted, "You never seem to amaze me with that gun Vince."

"That critter was ready to make a bad day for me. Thanks friend."

His horse had run down the trail for a ways before stopping. Jumping on the wagon we rode till we came up on him. He was pulling up on a patch of grass acting like nothing had happened.

"I'm lucky he still ain't running full out," speaking low with a sign of relief. "He's been pretty faithful to me for the most part."

Faithful until he went to grab for the reins, taking three tries and about a hundred feet before he had hold of him. It was kind of comical. We both got a pretty good laugh of it helping to forget what just occurred.

"We're laughing again when I should be thanking the lucky stars," Jeb announced.

I just shook my head, teasing, "Let's see how far we and faithful can get before dark."

"I think I'll ride with you in the wagon for a while," speaking as he tied his horse to the wagon.

Darkness came faster than we wanted. We found a comfortable looking spot just off the trail. It was a pretty grassy area with a stream laboring its way along the bank of a small hill. The horses didn't mind the chance to get a stomach full of cool fresh water. Jeb and I found no complaints either. At one section there was a small shallow pool enough for a much needed bath. Each taking turns we jumped in, washed, and jumped out, diving for our blankets before freezing to death.

Thinking we were but a day away from the next town and civilization, I anticipated a place to search with hopes of finding something. We settled down with a small fire and had a pot of beef stew Jeb had cooked up. He had gotten the ingredients at the last supply stop. It was all he talked of since. Saying it was his favorite. Something about the way his mother made it and taught him the ingredients and how long to cook it. He said the longer it simmered the better it held the flavor.

It looked like basic flour, water, beef and vegetables to me. I always watched my dad make it and it always tasted the same. Not to hurt Jeb's feelings, I mentioned nothing of it. It was good, warming and filling our bellies.

"One thing I miss is good home cooking," he said while wiping up the last of the gravy with his biscuit.

The rest of the night was uneventful until morning when we heard the sound of many hooves stomping in the far-off trail. Finishing breakfast we were packing and getting ready to start a new day. Jeb decided to ride the wagon giving his horse a break and run along side Colt.

Within minutes, we saw the stage laboring its way up a long slanted trail heading east.

"It's pretty early to see a stage, eh Jeb?"

"There must be a town right close," I guessed.

"Good, maybe you'll find some more home cooking sooner than you expected Jeb," I chuckled.

Thinking always fascinates me when I (think) about something. The brain is an amazing tool. It doesn't matter what subject enters one's mind, the brain picks up everything it knows about it. Food for instance, cooking, hunger, what to eat to satisfy ones taste and which ones don't. Guns, rifle or pistol, make, model, careful aim with a rifle, quick draw it accuracy. Cleaning and caring for the weapon. Life, living or dying, how to survive the day, live, love, travel, settle down. Women, when's the next time you'll meet one, where, under what circumstances, blonde, black hair, shapely, smile, and carefree or hurt or distraught. Mission, when, where, how, talk or action.

See? No matter what subject enters one's mind begins to work.

My mind was now on a mission, - mine, getting frustrated wanting to find this killer, being able to find him, when, where, will I kill him or will I be killed? Don't be ridiculous, I will find and destroy! No matter how long it takes. What will I do after this is all over? Could I go back to the ranch with what has happened to my family? Will I stay out west? Will I find a woman, marry, and raise a family? Will I just ride and wander exploring the country?

"Jeb," I broke the silence to get away from the thinking that was smothering me. "It's getting colder every day. Winter's on its way. Nights and mornings are cooler and the rains colder."

"Yep," was his answer.

I guess he was deep in thought as I had been.

Was I ready to travel throughout the winter or should I think about holding up in the next town. I needed to sell the wagon at the next town and go horse back so we could move further faster, take short cuts where a wagon couldn't. Supplies carried on our horses were all we'd have.

When was Jeb going to get to his destination? Would he hold up through the winter with me or wish to continue?

I knew the day would come when he found his kin and we would be saying our good-byes.

Next thing I knew, we were staring down at the biggest town I'd ever seen since we left home. It seemed more like a city with a large population.

Chapter 8

Riding into town, we passed the sign "Welcome to White Water." We blended in with all the other riders and wagons. People were crowding the sidewalks, crossing the streets, kids running, dogs following. There at an intersection was a medicine wagon with the healer selling his goods out the back of it. He was saving all the good souls with his magic Indian potion while relieving them of their hard earned money. People were busy going everywhere and anywhere. I never saw such a busy place.

"Let's get the horses watered."

"K," I answered.

Pulling up to the water trough in front of the feed store, the horses wasted no time quenching their thirst. The trough was well cared for. You could see a drain, handle, and pump. Anyone could see it must have been serviced frequently.

Hopefully I'll get some answers or at least some helpful information here. Staying for the winter probably wouldn't be a bad idea. This place seemed to have everything. There were stores lined up one side and down the other.

"Beer partner?" said an enthusiastic Jeb.

"Twisting my arm," I answered.

Tying the horses to the rail, we got down. I gave a quick glance around which was a habit now. A quick familiarization of the surrounding area never hurt, it could keep you from being killed.

When we walked through the bat wings, you would have thought it was a Friday night.

"Two beers," I yelled to the bartender as we settled up against the bar.

"Is it always this crowded this early in the day?" I asked as the tender set two mugs down.

"More than I can keep up with, business is good," he stated. "I hear there's a herd of 8000 head on the outskirts of town. I spect to be getting even busier when them cow hands get into town. Weather's treacherous northwest where they're heading," speaking as he wiped the bar top. "Guess they'll be waiting out the storm some before getting underway. Haven't seen you two around, you riding through?"

"Don't know yet," Jeb answered. "Just like the cattlemen, have to see what the weather has in store. This may be a good place to hold up for a while."

"Carson's the name," the bartender announced. "White Water's a pretty nice town. I rode in for supplies heading west and that was five years ago."

"Jeb, Vince," Jeb said nodding to me.

"Glad to meet you fellas," looking inquisitively. "You two aren't lawmen are you?"

"No, why would you ask?" I questioned.

"This town's getting a little crazy with all these drinkers. We only have one sheriff and one dumb deputy," he said with a concerned low tone.

"Are you hinting we should look into hiring on as lawmen?" Jeb asked.

"If you're good with a gun and not wanted, the job would be a sure thing; sheriff said so." he answered.

"You must be expecting trouble?" I questioned again.

"Come Friday night there will be many men cramming in for their drinking and cards. There's my place and the Sun Palace down the street. Poker players there will be plenty. Not so for the women working these two places. You figure it out."

"Been much trouble lately?" Jeb asked.

"No, but that's what concerns the sheriff. It only takes one drunk cowhand to collide with the wrong miner or jealous one over a women and all hell could break loose."

"See what you mean," I answered.

"Well, I guess we'll just fend for ourselves for the time being." Jeb barked as he looked around.

Locating an open poker table for two in the back he grabbed me and said, "Let's play a little if they'll let us in," carrying his glass and pulling me at the same time.

"Room for two more players?" asking as we walked over to the table of three.

"Sure, sit, always room for two more to throw in some dough for the needy," he said with a friendly smile.

I sat down in a chair which faced the rest of the room; this made me comfortable in case trouble should occur. Jeb sat next to me, but not quite as good an angle.

The three men introduced themselves; we introduced with first names only and commenced playing. Three or four hands into the game, two beers appeared in front of Jeb and me. I looked up to a quite good looking young lady.

"Hey boys," I'm Jamie and I'm going to be taking care of you tonight."

I handed her two bits and answered, "Good meeting you, Jamie, I'm Vince and that there ugly one is Jeb. We'll be your customers tonight."

"What a pal," Jeb snarled back.

"You two just get in?" Jamie asked.

"Just a few hours ago," I answered.

"Where you staying?" she asked with a sexy smile.

"I reckon just outside of town," I answered.

"Nonsense, two good looking guys like you need a nice room," she winked at me, then glancing over at Jeb. "I reserved a room for my brother who was supposed to be in town today, but I got word earlier he won't be here for two more days. Pay me two dollars the room's yours. Upstairs, go right, second door on the left facing the street."

Watching these three, they seemed innocent enough and I didn't detect any signs of cheating, so I kicked my feet back and relaxed for an evening of cards. Conversation was easy and the playing field never got out of hand, even though my winnings were slight. Jeb was about forty bucks to the good by the end of the evening. We learned that these three had ended here with a wagon train from the East along with their families. Having traveled three months to reach this destination, they were satisfied to hold up here and try mining hoping to strike it rich like all the other miners in town.

"How about you boys? What's your story?" one asked.

"Looking to meet up with my two brothers in Colorado," Jeb said. "Vince here is my riding partner."

That's all that got said. I didn't want to explain my presence to anyone if I didn't have to.

As I had glanced around the room watching the men playing cards or loitering against the bar, I could see where a sheriff with only one deputy could be a little worried. More than once I noticed where trouble could easily breakout.

There were as many as a dozen men that looked like a couple of ornery polecats that would jump to instigate trouble at any time. Those I would stay clear of but would be curious enough to find more about them as time went on.

The next few nights I would watch and listen.

Maybe someone will know something. Maybe it was one of these rough riders I'm looking for, maybe one of these men I will kill.

"I'm gonna call it a night," announced one of the three," I believe his name was Jack, "So if you gentlemen will excuse me." Scraping up his few bucks on the table, he tipped his hat and left.

"Nice fella," Jeb commented.

"Not a regular, but sits in with us from time to time," the man called Bob stated as he shuffled the cards.

Before Bob could begin dealing, a big dark shadow appeared over the vacant chair.

"Mind if I sit in?" a low rough voice filled the air.

I looked up into the eyes of one big, ugly rough looking man.

"Have a seat," Bob answered politely.

The stranger sat, reached into his jacket pocket and laid down a handful of bills.

"What's your poison friend?" he asked.

"Five card stud," Bob answered again.

I noticed his eyes going from each of us at the table. Cold looking that put me on alert. This man was definitely a gunslinger, a killer by nature. He had a face that looked chiseled One that would be hard to handle using fists.

I wondered if Jeb and I should have excused ourselves, but I was too curious to see out a few hands and what would pan out.

"Dick Murdocks the name," he stated like that should mean something to us.

Maybe it did, but I never heard the name in my travels. It sounded as if he may have grace his likes on a wanted poster. Maybe bragging how much a reward on his head?

As Murdock picked up his cards, he looked around. My guess was he was learning to read the expressions on the faces of each man as they played. He wasn't a stranger to a poker table either as he studied the face of each of us. Maybe he was looking to see if any of us could be a threat to him. Heck I was just playing to pass time away, lucky I was breaking even. Jeb was a little more serious showing the most winnings laid out in front of him. He had quite a stack in front of him. Murdock picked up on that too. After just a few hands, Jeb's pile was dwindling. He seemed to want to play out Murdock. I folded early unless I knew the cards were definitely in my favor. I continued to stay fairly even. I had an uneasy feeling all the time we were playing. That feeling was answered just a few more hands into the game.

As it happened to be, Murdock was shuffling the cards. Suddenly, as he was to start dealing, a black hat with a silver studded band flew and landed in the middle of the table upsetting the pile of money. You could see that Murdock recognized it immediately.

"Get up and walk outside really easy like, Murdock," ordered the voice from a young man standing from the side of where Murdock and I were sitting.

"I'd kill you right here," the young man's voice fired, "But I'm gonna kill you nice and easy, not like the half chance you gave my brother."

Murdock stood up looking at each of us and then to his challenger.

"Keep my place open. This shouldn't take long," he said with confidence.

We sat there and watched the two walk outside, the young fellow keeping some distance behind Murdock.

The saloon was thinning out. You could tell the street would be the same. Everyone knew there was going to be a gunfight and none wished to be hit by a stray bullet. Not even a minute later we heard the gun fire, two shots close together. The echo of the gun blast filled the streets and continued throughout the saloon.

About a minute later, a tall lanky man walked up to our table.

"If you were waiting for your friend to come back, you can just continue without him. He won't be," the patron announced with excitement in his voice. "Your friend wasn't as fast or as accurate; there's quite a hole in his throat."

"And the other man?" Bob asked.

"Not a scratch; just holstered his gun and walked to the sheriff's office," he reported.

"Come on Jeb, that's our cue to call it a night."

Jeb stood up folding his winnings tucking it in his inside vest pocket.

"Thanks fellas. Wonder what that was all about?" he asked.

"Can't rightly guess, I'm sure we'll find out come morning."

Too tired to reason or guess things out we were ready to go to the room which was offered to us. The room that sounded too good was just that, but it was worth the two dollars being that I was too tired to ride out and look for a place this late anyway.

"I'll take the horses to the livery, Jeb." I offered.

"Ok, I'll wait up for ya, thanks," he returned with a smile.

When I got back, I heard him snoring even before I got the door open.

Morning came fast. Sunlight was pouring through the thin curtains.

Jeb and I were up, dressed, and on our way to the lobby for breakfast. The tables were already half occupied. This was a week day which amazed me how busy it was. Most of the patrons were having full breakfasts not just coffee.

We sat down at a table against the wall and were greeted almost immediately with two mugs of coffee and a big friendly smile.

"Good morning, Jamie," I greeted.

"Oh," she replied. "I think you have me mixed up with my twin sister, sir."

If there was a way of telling these two apart, I sure couldn't see it.

"Two beautiful ladies identical in this town?" I snickered, and blushed.

"Put us side by side and you'd be amazed how hard it is to tell us apart," still smiling, "but if you stick around for any time, you'll get to know the difference. My name is Jane."

"Jamie and Janie," I kidded.

"Jane if you please, just Jane."

"Excuse me, Jane," I apologized. "Made me feel like a jerk."

Jeb and I ordered our breakfast and commenced to enjoy the coffee.

"Got put in your place, heh pal?" funned Jeb.

"Guess so," answering still embarrassed.

We listened to the silver banging and scraping the plates. Buzzing could be heard throughout the room of the gunfight last night. I guess that's a common entertainment in this town. Maybe that should make us think before we decide to stay in this town for the winter. We sure don't want to get involved in any trouble while we're here.

Sitting across the room with a young lady was the man who was in the gunfight last night. She seemed to be memorized by his style as they he talked while they ate. He looked like a real gentleman sitting there, cool, calm and collected, giving the lady his full attention.

"Look there Jeb, there's the hombre that killed Murdock."

Overheard by the man to my back, he turned and apologized, "I didn't mean to ease drop partner, but that there is Kid Stevens. Both Murdock and Stevens are known gunfighters in this territory or should I say Murdock was. Talk has it that Murdock shot Kid's brother in Dayton about a month back. Murdock said the brother was cheating at cards. His story was that when he was challenged, Kid's brother drew first so he cut him down claiming self-defense. Kid said his brother wasn't a gunfighter and had no chance no way."

With Murdock's reputation, no one seemed to challenge his story so he was told to leave town with no other action brought against him. That is, not until Kid caught up with him.

Witnesses said last night's gunfight was fair. Neither said a word, just stared for a few seconds and both hit leather together. When a professional gunfighter was going into battle there was seldom a conversation between the two. Their reputation spoke all that was needed when they were face to face in a gunfight that was going to be a sure thing.

They said that Murdock's head looked like it was falling off as the bullet took out his neck bone. It fell off to the side when the support was gone. It was actually sad to see a man brake like that in front of such and audience. The challenger showed no remorse as he slid his pistol back to the holster.

Kid yelled, "Now you went up against a real gun."

I don't think Murdock heard him though.

"They said they were both lighting fast, cleared leather, and fired at the same time."

I looked at this fella and said, "It's one thing to be fast mister; it's another to be accurate. Sometimes it's worth giving a split second for accuracy to hit your target."

"Well, sir," he remarked softly, "It wouldn't matter either way the Kid had him covered no matter which way."

I looked over at Kid Stevens. He looked no older than eighteen, long blond hair, medium build, and looked unconcerned about last night's dealings with the gunman they called Murdock.

As the man turned back, Jane was setting our breakfast down.

I looked up just in time to watch Kid Stevens get up to leave. He was noticeably neat like someone out of a Wild Bill Hickok western show, but he was obliviously someone who could back his showmanship up. He wore twin colts butt first. The right holster was tied down with the other tie hanging freely. He didn't seem like a cocky critter either. He was obviously brought up educated with manners and used them as he excused himself from the lady. He used his napkin to dab his mouth with instead of wiping. He left trying not to attract attention but that was impossible. It seemed everyone hushed till he exited, and then the buzz went on like nobody's business.

Jeb had little to say.

We finished our breakfast. Jane brought us both another hot mug of coffee and we sat back and let the food settle.

"I"ve been thinking of leaving Vince; this is just too much action for me. This town is too rowdy for my blood, and I don't wish to get myself caught up in something I'm not looking too," he announced.

"Can't much blame you, whatever you decide. I'm gonna to hang around for a while and see if I can find out anything about this man I'm hunting."

"I haven't made up my mind yet, but if I do go or hear anything at all, I'll get word back to ya," he promised.

"Thanks Jeb, you've been a good friend, I'm really glad we met up," I confessed.

"That goes for me too. I couldn't think of a better man to travel with, helped time to go by fast," he complimented.

"Let's cross that bridge when we get to it?"

"Deal."

Jane set down two more cups of coffee in front of us.

"How you two doing?" she asked with that sexy smile. "Do hope I'll see you for lunch."

"Time will tell pretty lady," I flirted back.

She squeezed my forearm which could be understood as a show of interest. I'd treat myself to lunch and see what that squeeze really meant.

"I'm gonna go down and pay a visit to the sheriff. Let him know of my purpose here in town," I rendered.

"You do that; I'm gonna stop by the stage depot and see what the traveling's like," Jeb added.

The sheriff's office was five buildings down on the opposite side of the street. I entered but no one was around. I walked over to check out the wanted posters. I remembered looking at the wanted posters as a kid whenever I accompanied my Dad to town. He would try to keep me next to him while conducting his business knowing I would some times have a night mare of one of the faces that would intimidate a young fella like me.

Mostly $100 rewards but always one or two for $500 to $1,000. That was a lot of money to have on one's head. There was also the job of bounty hunters who thought so too. Bounty hunters had to be as much outlaw as the outlaw they hunted. You had to think as an outlaw, dress like an outlaw, travel the same trails as an outlaw. But most of all, be better with a gun than an outlaw.

I was looking at a $100 poster surprised to see a young lady's face when the sheriff walked in. Mary Roberts was a young pretty woman wanted for robbing a stagecoach of a payroll delivery.

The door opened and I heard the steps of two men enter. Turning I saw the Sheriff followed by his deputy.

"Morning," he said as he laid his rifle down across the desk. Behind him a much younger fellow with a badge on his coat pocket, "Can sure tell winter's coming."

"Sure can," I answered. "Colder each morning."

"You here about last night's shooting?" he questioned.

"Not really, Murdock was playing at our table last night but I don't know anything else," I surrendered.

"What can I do for you, young fella?" he asked looking at me from head to toe.

"Call me Vince please."

"Ok, you can call me Pat; what can I do for you, Vince?" he came back.

"I'm hunting a man who killed my family a few months back. I believe he may be headed west. He could be holding up here as I am with the weather and all, yet, could have traveled through already."

"Do you have a name or description of the fellow, Vince?" he asked.

"No, and that's the problem. The only clues were a broken shoe on the mare he rode and a livery man remembering reshoeing such a horse. He did give a sketchy description of the rider. Murdock fit that description, but he came from the north I've found out."

"Sounds like you're looking for a needle in a haystack partner."

I stood there with a blank look on my face. He was right; in this place there were a hundred men that fit that description. Many of the men looked dangerous moving about town with suspicion of anyone who paid them any mind.

"I hope he makes the mistake of getting drunk and blabbing where he's from," I said. "That would at least get my attention and give me some hope."

"And where is your home town?" he asked.

"Pinewood, Pinewood, Arkansas," I answered, thinking it wasn't any of his business.

"Most we can do is keep our eyes and ears open, Vince. If we come up with something we'll let you know. One thing Vince, I want no gunplay or a vigilante in this town, savvy?" he warned.

"Savvy," I answered.

I turned heel and headed out the door. Walking down the walkway, I thought day time was not the best time for investigating. My answers would come at night. The type of man I was looking for would probably be sleeping off the night before.

I thought I'd take a ride outside town, sort things out, and clear my head and give Colt some time to run off some of his stored up energy.

Chapter 9

As I stepped from the last building to an alleyway that separated the livery, I heard a gunshot and found myself dropping to the ground. The swish of the bullet passing by me sounded like a big bumblebee which ripped and carried away part of the collar of my coat leaving a warm sensation on my neck.

I stayed down, not only from the surprise attack, but to also play possum. A few seconds later, a man ran up from the alley, then others from all other directions. I glanced up with my gun drawn seeing that the man was unarmed. Men started to move closer now that they knew it was safe. Not wanting a lot of attention I shook it off and stood up wiping the dust from my clothes.

"I came up on the shooter startling him, mister. When he saw me, he high tailed it shooting at the same time," a stranger reported.

"Well mister, you may have just saved my life," I answered humbly.

"My name is Cole," he stuttered

"Vince," I introduced, "Thanks Cole, you just saved my skin."

By now the sheriff was next to me looking where the bullet tore my collar. Seeing that I was the victim he looked up and down the street as if he was going to see the shooter just standing there waiting to be arrested.

Looking at the man who just finished talking to me, he asked, "Can you give me a description mister?" he asked.

The shaky man started hyperventilating from what he had just witnessed. He could have been shot as easily for recognizing the shooter.

"Catch your breath mister, can I help you?" I said concerned.

"Just give me a minute," his quivering voice labored out.

I knew now I was on the right trail.

"I want you both to come with me back to the office," the sheriff said with a stern voice. "Someone has to know something about this. Break it up and go home everyone unless you have something to tell me," he ordered the crowd of men hanging about.

"You're both pretty lucky fellows for being at the wrong place at the wrong time."

I thought to myself, this witness was at the right place at the right time, or I'd be dead now. I may also get my first real clue to which I was searching for.

Jeb came running up, "What in tar nation happened? You all right?" he yelled.

"You recognized the man in the alley, Cole?" the sheriff asked.

"I think so, but to describe him would be describing most of the men in town," he answered.

"That's not much to go on," he retorted.

"I'm sorry, if I run into him on the street, I'll fetch you," he promised.

"Well, be careful Cole," the sheriff warned, "If you recognized him, then there is a big chance he recognized you."

"Come on Cole, let me buy you a beer," I offered.

"Whiskey," Cole answered, "I like whiskey."

"Whisky it is."

Cole wasn't one to like to sit. He liked leaning on the bar. I didn't feel much like sitting either. I could watch my back in the mirror that graced the back of the bar facing the bat doors. I felt safe now with Jeb at my side.

"So what brought you to the back alley, Cole?" I asked.

"Well, I live six cabins back. That's my way into town," answering with the anticipation of whiskey.

"Lucky for me."

"Whose feathers did you ruffle mister?" as he waved the bartender over.

I ordered a whiskey and two beers. When they were set in front of us, I laid down a dollar. The drinks would serve more as a sedative hopefully to settle my nerves. The more I thought about it the more I realized how lucky I was. If the shooter had waited just a bit longer and took his time with the shot, I would have been dead right now.

"I'm hunting a man Cole, a man that killed my family back East. I guessed he traveled west, now maybe I think I guessed right." I finally responded to his question.

"Do you know this man? Does he know you're following him?" he asked with caution.

"Til now, only a hunch. I wouldn't think he'd know he was being hunted. Unless he knew my whole family and knew he didn't cash my chips in at the time. If you can find this fella again and point him out to me, maybe then I can settle this once and for all. See you later Cole." I answered turning heel heading for the door with my friend next to me.

Jeb and I cautiously walked through the bat wings and gave a quick glance through out the area looking for anything suspicious.

"What do you think, Vince? Believe this guy?" Jeb asked with concern.

"The man doesn't even wear a gun, but I'm gonna play it cautious with everyone till I can find out differently," answering with caution. "Night time I could understand, but to try to kill a man in broad daylight don't make much sense. Hired gun or your man you search for? What do you think?" I asked.

"Damn coward," he sneered. "Money, a man will do just about anything or take a chance like that for money."

I looked up to the sky. A few clouds tarnished a perfectly blue sky. To myself, I was thanking the man upstairs that I was still here to enjoy this day.

"I was on my way for a ride, so I guess I'll just saddle up and do so. Maybe this polecat will follow. I'll be ready now," I announced.

"I'll stay back and see if anyone is interested in what you're doing," he offered.

"Thanks Jeb."

Colt was glad to see me. He was ready for a run.

While I was saddling the paint, I could feel his muscles twitching, his breathing picking up as his heart beat. His eyes followed me as I moved about. He was one fine horse and he was like family. As I spoke to him, his ears would perk turning his head with my movements. After I slid my Winchester into the sheath, I grabbed the bridle and led him outside.

I threw my left foot up into the sturip and swung up into the saddle. I knew what was coming next so I grabbed the reins and hung on. This fella didn't need no spurring. For the first 50 feet, he was like an unridden bronc. I think he just wanted to assure me, I was the only rider he would allow to mount and ride. I knew his moves like a dancing partner; if a horse could smile, I knew he was each time I mounted him. Off we went, out of town like a bullet. I gave him full rein and let him do as he pleased. Not only was he fast, but he had the smoothest stride of any horse I'd ridden.

A mile or so I picked a trail that would take me out in open territory. If someone was to follow, he would be in clear sight. I slowed the paint down and brought him around so I could view a full 360 degrees. It wasn't long before I knew no one was coming. I looked hard, hoping to discover the truth. Wishing to end this so I could get back to a normal life.

The day was too nice. I knew there was nothing in town of interest until evening. I rode to an area that I discovered as we rode into this town. A green area where I knew there would be a pond, lake, or at least a stream. I was right. So much green with a pretty fair sized pond, fed by a spring, the water was clear and cool.

Colt enjoyed all the cool water and green grass his belly could hold. It was a good time to clear my mind and relax. I would soon return to continue my search. I thought of Jane, her smile, beauty, and her hand touching my arm. A short time after, Colt was as ready as I and had me back to town in time for lunch.

As I walked into the restaurant, the first person I saw was Jane. Our eyes met at the same time, darn she was beautiful. Our smiles must have surfaced in sequences.

"Hi Vince, I'm so glad you came. Come sit, I have a table waiting for you," she said enthusiastically. "What happen to you I was so scared, I can't have anything happen to my new friend, that would be such a shame."

Her eyes were as blue as a cloudless sky, blond hair as long and straight as a well- groomed Palomino's mane, about the best hour-glass figure I'd seen on any woman I'd ever met. I swear this woman had the voice of an angel and a body that seemed to float in the air with her every move. Why she took favor to me was a mystery in itself.

"What's your pleasure honey?" her voice accompanied with that beautiful smile.

"How bout a steak that's still breathing, potatoes, whatever greens you're serving and some bread," I answered.

"That sounds more like dinner than lunch," she kidded.

"Well this may be my dinner also. I think I'm gonna be too busy tonight for eating." I confessed.

"Well, I get off at nine. I hope you can find some time for me in between or after your business," she invited.

"I'll find the time," I promised.

My meal showed up within the half hour. I don't mind saying, hats off to the cook. It's been a while since I had a meal fixed so well. As I was finishing my last bite when a serving of rhubarb pie was set down in front of me.

"This is on the house honey," she offered with that cute smile and a breath taking wink.

It was hot, not even time to cool down, and it was good. I Remembered how good Marge's pies were, and remembered her smile as she served the fresh baked pies after dinner. Now it was to be no more.

It was getting late, the room was emptying out. Jane came and asked if she could sit with me a spell. I was honored and stood up, pulling a chair for her. We spent the next hour talking, getting to know one another.

One thing I learned was how disappointed she was in how her sister Jamie working in the saloon. How men thought they could come to the restaurant and handle Jane like they were accustomed to handling saloon gals.

I stated my thoughts and concerns which were sincere but hoping I wasn't over stepping my boundaries.

"I've asked her to quit many times, but she refuses to even look for different work," she sadly said. "She won't talk to me for a while when I bring it up so I try my best to hold my tongue when I feel like speaking.

"It's her decision Jane, if that's what she wishes to do, you best accept it or chance losing her as a sister," I cautioned.

I finished the last bite of pie I was savoring, washing it down with the last of my coffee. I wiped my mouth and excused myself.

I turned to face the door wondering who could be outside waiting for me. Maybe I was being paranoid. I'd rather be cautious than dead. Dropping my hand to my pistol butt, I pulled it up from the holster then let it drop back in lightly. If I needed it, this would be no time to have it stick.

As I walked out, I saw the sheriff across the street talking to two pretty young ladies which gave me a sigh of relief.

When he looked up and saw me, he tipped his hat to the ladies and headed my way.

"Vince, may I call you Vince?" he politely asking.

"You may," I conceded. "As long as I don't have to call you Sheriff."

"Bill, call me Bill," he answered. "Word has it these cowboys are leaving tomorrow to take their herd north. They believe they can get to their destination before any big blizzard hits. My problem is in four days. There's gonna be another herd coming up from Texas and the cowhands coming in won't be heading on until winter breaks."

"And your point is?" I asked knowing what was on his mind and ready to expect the favor he was about to ask.

"My point, Vince, is this. I'd like you to consider hiring on as my deputy if you're going to wait out the winter. You might even be safer if your seen walking with a badge. If you're attacked, the penalty is sure stiffer if you're a lawman than just a citizen."

"Sheriff, if I get shot by a gunman, I'm gonna be just as dead with a badge as without, so why should I care," I confessed.

"If you're seen with a badge it may make a fellow think twice before he tries to put you down. Don't you see? You're a good man Vince. I could sure use your help. We can help each other. It pays $40 a month and a roof over your head with meals," he pleaded.

"If Jeb is to move on as he says he is, I'll take the job but just till winter's end or I find information on the man I'm looking for. I may have to leave on a moment's notice," I said sparingly.

"It's a deal," he said, reaching to shake my hand. I could see in his eyes he was desperate.

I started wondering how good with a gun this man was, or his one deputy. Was I being hired as a deputy or a bodyguard for these two? If I signed on, would this sheriff put more effort in helping me gain information? This could be an asset in other ways for me.

If these cowhands were heading on tomorrow, tonight would be their last night to tie on a good one. Once they hit the trail, liquor was not welcome to come along. This could be a hell of a night.

I thought to myself this town would thin out quite a bit for four days. That would give me some time to sort out some of the men who remain. Then I thought would the killer be riding with the herd?

Everything was spinning in my mind again. What should I do? Will I ever catch up to the killer, or was I wasting my time?

I looked to my friends, the law, even prayed to God to help me put to rest this agonizing nightmare.

Remembering something my dad always told us, "Things have a way of working out. Time given, questions and problems will be solved."

Rolling a cigarette, I led Colt down to the livery. I wouldn't be riding anymore today. I walked, glancing down each alley as I passed by. There were two.

As I led Colt into the barn, I noticed the fanciest saddle and bridle I'd ever seen. It was star studded up one side and down the other, the bridle was a match. I didn't have to wonder who this belonged to as I remembered the holster belt Kid Stevens was wearing. All made by the same leather craftsman.

I could just imagine the cost of such. As I jested to the livery man, he pointed to Kid's horse. He was just as magnificent as Colt.

When I finished, I walked back down to the saloon to meet up with Jeb. Pushing through the bat door, I could see him already engrossed in a poker game with a stack of bills in front of him.

"Hey Vince, have a seat. Honey, bring Vince a beer please," shouting to one of the saloon gals.

The three men sitting at the table were strangers to me but looked on the up and up. Stories were being told, men were laughing, and having a good time. Jeb was a pretty good judge of character so I guess that was how he found these men to hang with.

"You still thinking of moving on partner?" I asked.

"Yes, I think I will," he answered. If I get underway now I have a chance of beating the bad weather. How about you?

"I'm gonna hang for a while. I have a feeling there's some answers to be had here. I must admit also I've taken a liking to Jane," I answered with a smile.

"She's reason enough to stay a while I'd say. I see the way she acts around you; I'd say she's taken quite a fancy to you too," he admitted.

Taking a few long gulps of my beer, I scanned the room taking in all the faces I could without raising suspicion.

Jamie caught my eye and gave me a wink even though she was busy with some customers at a table across the room. She was as pretty as her sister, lighting up the room as if you were standing out in the sun. Her hair as straight and golden as all get out. I could just sit there and let my eyes eat up all that beauty for hours. The two men she was entertaining must have felt the same way as they weren't having much trouble throwing down money to keep her company. She was trying to pick out the better of the crowd and shying away from the rowdies.

Chapter 10

As I finished my beer, the back door swung open and Kid Stevens appeared.

He stopped, scanned the room, and walked over to the bar.

"Good looking horse mister," slurring as he walked by.

"Let me buy you a drink," I offered.

"That paint looks like it came from good stock," commented Kid.

"Yes sir, he came from a darn good blood line," I confessed.

Kid motioned for two drinks to the tender.

"Leave the bottle," he ordered.

The tender set down two glasses and the whiskey.

Standing alone with no one beside us to hear, Kid asked, "Who you gonna leave that horse to when you die?"

"Well now, what do you mean by that?" I inquired.

"I've been paid to kill ya and I always do what I'm paid for," he confessed.

A hired gun. I should have figured. New fancy clothes always clean. No signs of a man who labored hard for money. Now I know how he paid to have such a fine horse and accessories.

"Kill me huh?" I asked sarcastically

"That's what I just said," he stated with confidence.

"Who hired you and why?" I asked calmly.

"What do you care? You're gonna be dead."

"I believe the man who hired you may be the coward who ambushed and killed my whole family back East, one of which was my kid sister of just sixteen!" I pressed.

Kid took his glass, gulped it, and refilled it.

"Take a drink mister, I'm not gonna kill ya right now. I am gonna kill ya, but I'd like to hear more of your story."

I took up my glass, sipped it, and set it back down. I then commenced telling my story. I could see in his eyes he was letting his brain take in all the information. When I was finished, I pleaded, "That's why I want to know the name."

"This does put a new light on things mister. I'm a fair man as I trust you are. Here's how it's gonna go down. I'm gonna be back later tonight to call you out. I'm gonna kill you right outside those doors with an audience to prove a fair fight. After I kill you and since I believe your story, I'm gonna kill this here man and you two can sort it out in the after life."

"And if you can't get the job done?" I asked.

"I'll tell you what. That ain't gonna happen. You're gonna be as dead as you're standing here. But just to be a player, I'll have the name written on a piece of paper in my shirt pocket. How's that for ya?"

Darn, this kid was so cool and sure of himself.

"If that's the only chance I'm offered to find this murdering coward, so be it," I surrendered.

"Tonight then," he commented.

I didn't finish my drink. I didn't need any more liquor in my body to slim my chances of survival. I turned heel and sat back down with Jeb.

This kid was no older than I. How can one be so sure of one self? Standing at the bar as bold as could he be sucking down a few more shots, throwing some coins on the bar, he turned and strutted out into the street.

If I survived this night, I would know who my prey was. Who was this cow dung? How much money was this to cost him? How did he know who I was or what I was after? Well, I was one shot away of finding out or one shot away of finding nothing out, and pushing up daisies.

Jeb looked over at me asking, "What'd you get yourself into now?"

I didn't hear the question. I was so deep in thought.

"Vince!" he spoke with authority.

"What," I retorted.

"You in trouble?"

"I'll tell you later."

I had a sick feeling in my lower gut like a stick of dynamite blowing off. I'd just as soon fight it out now and get it over with. Did Kid's stomach feel as mine? Why tonight? Why not right then?

"Jeb, I'm going up to the room," saying as I got up, "Speak with you in a while."

I got to the room and laid down. Now my head was starting to hurt. I sat up and moved the table which stood at the side of the room.

I pulled my pistols, discharged the six cartridges from each of the cylinders, and broke down the guns to clean them. These were the new colts given to me by my dad. I carried the best gun cleaning kit money could buy. Keeping my mind busy relieved the knotting pain in my stomach and the headache I was experiencing.

I proceeded to reassemble the guns and reinserted the cartridges. If I do draw faster, aim better, the last thing I would need would be a misfire.

Jeb showed himself to the room about the time I finished with my gun carrying quite a roll of bills.

"Had yourself a good afternoon at the tables, aye, partner?" I congratulated.

"Never mind me, word travels fast in this town," he questioned, "What have you gotten yourself into?"

"A showdown with Kid Stevens," I murmured back with a hard stare.

"I don't know about this, Vince. He's supposed to be a real bad dude with a gun," he stated with concern.

"I didn't seem to have much choice, he called me out," I said with anger.

"How about going to the sheriff? I'm sure he would stop this nonsense," he offered.

"He'd probably get himself killed if he meddled," I answered looking up at him. "It would only prolong Kid's intentions. He was hired by the man I'm looking for. This fight is inevitable. Win or loose, the man I've been looking for is going to die."

"How you figure?" he asked.

"If Steven's is to take me down, he promised to kill the man who hired him. He won't give me his name. Now if I survive, the name of this stranger will be written on a piece of paper in Steven's shirt pocket. Then I get the name and I'll know who I'm hunting."

"What can I do Vince?" he asked with concern.

"Nothing, just hang back and see how this thing plays out," I answered hoping of course I would prevail.

Looking up to the heavens, I prayed my family would look down on me giving me the strength and courage I needed to get through this.

How fast the darkness closed in. I was so busy in thought I lost all track of time. If I was ever ready for anything so important in my life, this was it. Killing a man to get what I needed didn't set well with me. If Dad were here with me, I'm sure he'd agree.

My headache diminished, but my stomach was knotted tighter than a cinch on a Brahma bull ready to be rid.

It was time to meet my challenger. I stood strapping my belt and tying the holster. I pulled my pistol and gave it a good going over, then slid it back in the holster lightly.

"I'm coming with you to keep things fair," Jeb announced.

I didn't answer, just gave a thankful nod as I opened the door to exit.

As we entered the hallway, the noise of the evening crowd was normal. It seemed no one knew what was about to happen. That would change soon, I thought. The piano was keying out a slow ballad with voices buzzing like a swarm of bees.

Stepping down the stairway to the bar, I was cautiously looking around for Stevens or anyone else who may have been hired to do some dirty work. Everyone seemed to be occupied with their drinking and card playing.

My stomach was in such pain. I thought if I took a bullet, I wouldn't even feel it. Standing at the bar looking up at the mirror I waited. Jeb was standing silently at my side alert as I'd ever seen him. The minutes seemed like hours waiting with anticipation for those bat wings to swing open. The door action seemed petty spaced out as most men entered for their evening of luck with the cards or beer to satisfy their thirst. I knew many tonight were here for their last night, leaving in the morning heading back to continue their cattle drive.

Then when I started to feel some relief, both doors swung open and Stevens came strutting in like the world should stop. It was like slow motion as he stepped closer to the bar. Swallowing hard, I took a deep breath and turned to face him. Darn we were close, I thought. At this distance we were probably going to both take lead. I knew there was no way out now.

"That name in your pocket?" I asked.

"It is," he answered. His eyes squinting showing he meant business. "Nothing more to say friend, draw, or I'm gonna kill ya where you stand."

The place was quite, hell it was now silent. He had just invited me to draw on him or to be killed. I thought this to be to my advantage. He was the professional gunfighter so I may need that split second to make it even. But would that be enough?

Without hesitation I slapped the grip of my pistol pulled and fired. I saw my gun belch flame with a puff of smoke. Steven's gun bellowed out but as he was still bringing it up to my level, his bullet entered the floor at my feet. Mine had already stuck him.

He looked down at the damage as he went down in disbelief. He looked up at me and my gun.

I walked over and knelt beside him ordering everyone away. "No one make a move," I ordered, reaching into his pocket I grabbed the paper I was looking for. It was there just as he said. Kidd Stevens was dead.

"Now you can do what you want," I told the crowd.

At that second Jeb was at my side along with the Sheriff.

"Well Jeb," I said, "This is the name of the man I'm after."

I stood unfolding the paper with endless anticipation. I thought my heart was coming out of my chest. I took a deep breath ready to discover who this man was.

It read: "Sorry friend, I really would have killed him as I promised. See you in hell!"

I couldn't believe this. He gave me his word.

I was so mad I ran over in desperation, pushing through the crowd, lifting his dead head, yelling "Who, who was he?" shaking him.

Blood was running out of his lifeless body.

"Who? Damn it!" I yelled to no avail.

A man now dead. How senseless, I thought. When a man gives his word, he's supposed to keep it.

"I would have shot him down had he killed you, Vince," Jeb responded.

"If you had, I would have had to arrest you," commented the Sheriff, "Good thing your friend prevailed. I'm sure there's a reward for this fella, dead or alive. Come see me in my office later," looking over at me.

Not caring I out gunned the great Kidd Stevens, I thought only how he betrayed me. He gave me his word. To me he was a no good skunk.

I ran back to the body. The sheriff was pushing everyone away. His boots were off and gone as well as his gun and holster. They would have left him stark naked had the sheriff not intervened.

"I want to go through his pockets," I pleaded.

"I'll do that mister, after I get him outta here. If there's anything you need to know, I'll find you." he promised.

What else could I say, "Thanks."

The street was clearing, some going back to the tables, some to the bar. The piano was even playing again. There was plenty of buzzing filling the room from some people who probably weren't even there.

Jeb followed me through the saloon and upstairs to my room.

Conversations ceased as we walked through the crowd heading up the stairs but commenced as we got to the top.

"Sorry Vince," Jeb said consoling.

"Damn him, damn him to hell!" I yelled.

"I'd say he's entering that territory as we speak," Jeb reassured me.

Chapter 11

There was a knock at the door, I looked to Jeb. "Only the sheriff," he warranted.

There was another man with him. Jeb stopped him to find out that he was with the town paper looking for a story.

"Beat it friend, or I'll break both your hands and you won't be writing about nothing," he warned as he slammed the door.

Minutes later there was another knock at the door, a bit more softly.

"It's Jamie," Jeb announced.

"Like hell, I'm Jane! Now let me in," Jane yelled in disgust.

Jeb opened the door. Jane came running to me with open arms, crying, "Thank God you're all right."

"That I am," I whispered, consoling her by rubbing my hand down the back of her head and down her long blonde hair, "Did you think it any other way?"

"Hold me Vince, just hold me," she begged.

"Jane, the newspaper man was here a few minutes ago. He cannot find out my name." I warned.

"Whatever you say. That will be easy since you never told me your last name any way," she answered teasingly.

Another knock came to the door. This time it was Jamie.

"I brought you a bottle. I thought you might need a drink to calm your nerves." she offered.

"Maybe one or two," but I don't think I need to drink myself into oblivion," I answered with gratitude.

There were two quick glances between the two girls.

"Sorry partner," Jeb apologized.

"I need to leave," Jane said, letting loose of a tight hug.

"Go on, I'll see you at breakfast," I retorted.

"Good night Vince," standing on her tip toes to get a kiss.

When Jeb and I were finally alone, the adrenaline rush dropped. I was feeling normal again.

"It's real important my name never gets out," I warned.

"You've got my sworn promise as a friend, and I believe that goes with the Sheriff also," he responded.

"If my name gets out, it would be from the man who hired Stevens. That would help me track him."

I laid down on the bed and was out like a light.

The next morning I woke to the noise of wagons leaving town. It was nice to be opening my eyes still alive. It was around 8:00 a.m. I had slept longer than I had wanted. My body must have needed the extra two hours to revive itself from the previous night.

I got up and rinsed my face. I looked out the window finding everything back to normal.

Getting dressed, I couldn't wait to get to breakfast.

It would be nice to see friendly faces.

Jeb was already seated and on his third cup of coffee staring at an empty plate.

"Morning," I gestured.

"Have a seat. I didn't wake ya knowing you needed the extra sleep," he confessed.

"Thanks, Jeb. I sure did." I responded.

Jane walked over to me from behind, put both hands on my shoulders, and squeezed.

''Good morning handsome," came that flirting voice.

"Good morning to you too," I returned.

"I'm going to fix you a special breakfast sweetie," she offered, "I hope you're hungry."

"About starved," I confessed.

She was off in a flash heading to the kitchen.

"You really are leaving, partner?" I asked.

"Yes sir, too much action for me to handle in this town," he confessed.

I looked around realizing it must have been a busy morning; there were many empty tables not yet cleared. I was glad most of the patrons were gone. I didn't need the attention of people buzzing gossip or pointing fingers while I ate. I would have liked breakfast in my room this morning, but I really wanted to see Jane's comforting smile to arouse this tired stressed body to act my blood flowing. It felt colder than yesterday. I hoped Jeb was making the right choice leaving so soon. One thing he didn't need was a blizzard as he was trying to scale the mountains.

There was no need trying to change his mind as I knew it would be useless. He had proved to be a real friend, and I was proud to have traveled with him. I hoped for him the best in finding his family safe.

The day flew by without incident or encounters with the Sheriff. I guess he found himself busy with other law business. I didn't think about the reward on Kid Stevens, but I was curious to see how much his reputation earned him as a hired assassin.

The next morning was even colder, so I decided to stay in.

Jane brought breakfast to the room just as I finished getting dressed. Knocking on the door, she walked in with a plate fit for a king eggs, potatoes, steak, biscuits and gravy.

"There love, how's this for a growing boy? I'll be back with a pot of coffee. Glad to see you a bit more cheerful," she said half giggly.

I stuck a napkin in my shirt, grabbed up a fork and knife, and dug in. Breakfast never tasted so good letting my stomach absorb each mouthful with pleasure.

Jeb watched me with surprise as I cleared the plate.

I saw him look up just as the Sheriff decided to pay us a visit. His voice was strong and sure as he came into the room.

"Morning fellas," he said as he threw his hat on a nearby chair. "Vince, I came by to let you know I checked all Stevens clothes, even went through his room. Whoever hired him must have sworn him to secrecy. I found nothing that would give a clue to who hired him. I'm sorry friend. Have you given any more thought to what we talked about?"

"I wasn't sure you'd still want me after what happened the other evening but if the offer still stands, I'll take it." I answered, "You must know now that I may have to leave in a moment's notice. If that's agreeable, you can swear me in later today."

Jeb was looking at me not saying a thing. I think he wanted to, but he would hold off till the Sheriff left.

"Come see me before lunch Vince and we'll do it. I need to go visit a few cow punchers who think they can have the run of the town," he said grabbing up his hat heading for the door.

I was right about Jeb holding his tongue.

The Sheriff didn't even clear the door before he lashed out, "What in Sams hell do you think your doing Vince?"

"This could work to my advantage," I defended, "I'll now have help in the territory and I'll be wearing a badge which gives me the authority to dig deeper into my investigation."

"Ever hear of dry gulching? That can happen to anyone who digs too deep," he added.

"That could happen with or without a badge." I answered, "Shouldn't you be getting ready to leave partner?"

"Trying to get rid of me, huh? Sounding too much like a mother?" he said before catching himself.

He sat quiet for a moment realizing what he had said, "Sorry Vince," he apologized.

"No apology needed," I answered.

I knew by how red his face was the embarrassment was enough.

"Vince," Jeb said sharply, "If you take this job as Deputy, your name will be in public records, something the news man would love to find out, then he could write the story of the year. Your name would be all over this territory.

"I didn't think of that, kinda puts a new outlook on the whole situation, huh?" I surrendered, "Guess I'll be declining the job."

"If the killer already knows you, then would it matter?" Jeb questioned.

"I don't know, I just don't know. I have till this evening to decide. I could care less if he knows my name. It's the territory I'm worried about. My Dad always warned me about getting a name for myself as a gunfighter. I know he was right. That's why I don't want my name reviled."

"You killed Kid Stevens," he warned, "You don't think that's gonna raise speculation of who the man is that outgunned him?"

"All more reason to keep my name secret," I replied.

Jane came over and sat next to me. I talked it over with her asking for advice. If I left it to her, I knew I wouldn't be taking the job either. I believed she'd be right too. I was lucky to have great friends. It was getting too confusing for me to make these decisions on my own.

I wanted to travel with Jeb, to see him find his family. I felt I owed that to him. Yet I wanted to stay right here with Jane. I knew I was falling for her. Staying here would have to be strictly my decision. I needed to find my killer. Was I letting my feelings for a woman get in the way of clear thinking? Tomorrow this town would have a 100 less men. I would have four days to investigate before more cowboys came to town. I would decline the Sheriff's offer later and say good-bye to my good friend in the morning. I would be with Jane for the next four days. After that, nothing was certain. I may have to leave town in a hurry even catch up to Jeb again.

The streets were beginning to thin out. The horses, pulling wagons and riders were vanishing, making the streets seem deserted.

Jeb would be gone in the morning, riding out in the safety of some of the cowboys. Somewhere along the trail he would have to split off and be on his own.

There wasn't too much talk of Indian trouble. The winter weather usually kept them hunting for food they would need to get through the winter. They didn't usually attack men in groups unless they outnumbered them. I would hope Jeb was far enough out of the Indian Territory before heading on his own.

The next two days were relatively quiet. I walked around town talking to different businessmen hoping someone would mention something. Most knowing of the gunfight shunned me as not wanting to get involved. I couldn't blame them.

The Sheriff wasn't happy with my decision, but understood my position. Bidding me well on my investigation, he promised to relay any information he may learn.

"Make sure you stay inside the law with your actions," he warned.

Today was Tuesday. I spent the afternoon with Jane. Fixing a picnic basket for us, we decided to take a horse and buggy out to the country. Finding an area with trees, grass, and a small stream, we decided this place to be the best.

Weather was getting cooler each day even with the sun doing its best to push its warm rays through. I started a small fire for warmth. We joked about this being the wrong time of year for a picnic, but agreed it was worth it. As she laid out the blanket, she surprised me by singing. Her voice was as lovely as she was. We ate and drank. Later we spent hours holding and caressing each other knowing how this time was precious. Not a care in the world, leaving all our problems on hold, even for a short time.

The sun set was so meaningful this evening. The cooler air surrounded us as the sun went down. This didn't bother us none. It was only a half hour ride back to town and with a couple of heavy blankets to lay over our laps, it was quite comfortable.

When we arrived back to town I thanked Jane for such a great day as I helped her off the buggy. She wrapped her arms around me giving me a great big kiss.

"You're so very welcome," she honored me, as she turned to go in. She made a few turns to assure me she was quite satisfied. "See you at breakfast honey," she said teasingly.

I returned the horse and buggy back to the livery throwing the tender a dollar.

Chapter 12

Thinking of the cold, I found myself concerned with Jeb's safety and pitied him for the decision he had made to leave to cross the mountains. I was glad I chose to stay longer. I could bath each night and know I'd have a warm bed to slip in.

It was a quiet evening; the untuned piano from the saloon filled the streets replacing the town's people who walked the boardwalks all day.

Pushing through the bat doors, I noticed the absence of many people. The cattlemen who chose to get the cattle through the mountains chancing the weather were now gone.

I walked up to the bar noticing the bartender had a beer waiting for me.

"Glad to see ya Vince," he spoke as he wiped the top of the bar trying to retain a shine that was years old.

Said his name was Al. I had taken a liking to him as I got to know him. Honest man, friendly to everyone deserving of it. He was very dedicated to his career and stayed out of everyone's business unless asked.

Finishing my second beer, getting ready to call it a night, a man came up and stood next to me.

"I know it's none of my business mister, but you may want to know what I overheard earlier," speaking in a loud whisper.

"And what would that be?" I asked.

"Al, how about a beer over here?" he called, "And one for this here fella too."

"No thanks mister," I answered, "I was just leaving. If you have something you want to tell me, spit it out."

Al set a beer in from of him. He downed it and set the empty glass down motioning for another.

"The name's Samuel, but my friends call me Sam," he announced as he reached out to shake.

"Glad to meet you Sam," I greeted shaking his hand, "Now what was it you wanted to tell me?"

"Last night I overheard a man trying to hire another to kill you. He said he didn't care how, just as long as you were eliminated," he offered, "They paid me no mind thinking I was drunk. The man who was offered the job quickly rejected the offer saying he was there when you killed that fella, Stevens. This other fella said nobody said anything about a fair gunfight. A back shoot would do just as well, paying the same. The fella called him crazy wishing him luck in finding anyone in town to take the job."

"That is news I should be aware of, Sam," I answered with gratuity, "Any description of either fella?"

"I didn't dare look at either. If they thought I overheard anything I could have been eliminated. But as a matter of fact, I did notice one of the fellas was scarred up on the face. His beard hid most of it, but it was still noticeable," he remarked.

Chapter 13

"You know darn good and well why we joined this here cattle drive Dave," growled Pat.

"$80,000 is being kept in this here mining town Whitewater. It's more than usual because of the mining but also the cattle drive that's headed this way," he announced.

Pat sat on the edge of a cut stump whittling the end of a stick with his pocket knife in deep thought. "$40,000 apiece he finally responded."

"We get the money and head west. Once over the mountains, no one will be brave enough to chase us, at least not til the weather changes. A posse just wouldn't risk chasing us fearing a storm. Most of the men have families and aren't paid enough to risk losing them because of a crumby snow storm or a bullet.

Still Pat sat listening silently whittling on that stick.

"That may be a good plan, but aren't we putting ourselves in the same danger trying to get away with the same chance of traveling in a horrid blizzard," he finally responded. "I don't have a family, but dead is dead any way you put it."

"Look, the way I have it panned is having a pack mule to carry plenty of supplies plus our horses. If we get snow on the way, it would surely cover our tracks making it almost impossible for a posse to follow unless they have an Indian tracker and that's not likely," Dave snarled.

Dave had it figured; both he and Pat would blend in with the other cattlemen when they got to town. Once there they could scope out the town, bank, and plan a fast get away. Killing for such a large amount of cash and gold would be a small sacrifice to the two killers. Both Dave and Pat were confident as they were both good with their guns.

The sky was pink and orange as the sun set. The evening was quiet as they elected to sleep a distance from the other cowpokes. Keeping with small talk, they hugged the campfire Pat had blazing to stay warm. A bath would be welcome as they had driven this herd hundreds of miles since the last town leaving them both smelling like an old grizzly.

Whitewater was about eight miles northwest. Knowing that, they figured on a good day.

Dave was figuring on pulling the job as soon as possible leaving little time for town's people to recognize them. One or two days would be enough time to explore and execute their mission.

That night they had both bedded down early and slept. Dave was awakened by Pat yelling in his sleep, "Watch out Dave, they've caught on to us, they have us surrounded. Dang! I've been shot! I've been shot!"

Dave slid over and kicked Pat about as hard as he could, "Wake up Pat! What in Sam's hell you doin'?" he growled at Dave in a low tone as not to wake the others, "You're talking in your sleep about our plans. Good thing we're away from the others, you'd had have us hung by morning!"

"Sorry Dave," Pat replied, rolling over falling back to sleep as fast as he'd been wakened.

Shaking his head, Dave pulled the blanket up trying to regain the warmth he had lost while waking Pat.

Lying there curled up he was thinking of the past. His brother had been killed two years earlier during a botched up robbery attempt. His brother Jim had hooked up with two sloppy bank robbers down Texas way. Staking out the town, they had discovered the town bank was holding a large stash of gold. Without much of a plan, they decided to just walk in and relieve the bank of all that gold in broad daylight. The timing couldn't have been worse. At this time a federal and territorial marshal were in the bank making a routine inspection.

Leaving one man out front to tend to the horses for the getaway, the other two stormed the bank. Kerchiefs pulled up covering their half face and guns drawn, they yelled to the teller to hand over the gold and cash. Hearing this, the two marshals came from the back where the safe was with their own guns drawn. Not expecting any of this, the two robbers were caught off guard. The only withdrawal they received was the lead from the Marshals guns. Dave's brother was able to get one shot off wounding one of the marshals but never knew it; he was dead before he hit the floor as his partner was. The man outside the bank was shot out of his saddle less than 200 feet away attempting his getaway.

Dave figured on being quite a bit more careful. His plan was to be aware of everyone's presence and hit the bank as it opened getting in and out quickly! He also slipped to sleep with- out realizing it.

Chapter 14

I woke to a still quiet morning with Jane next to me.

"Wake up darling, you're late, customers are waiting," I teased.

Wiping the sleep from her eyes, she sat up just to fall back on the mattress moaning, "Why don't we just stay in bed all day."

"No, No," I answered, "Get up." Pulling on her arms bringing her to a sitting position.

Laughing like a couple of little kids we got up, dressed, and headed downstairs. I was heading down for breakfast, and she hurrying off to work.

The aroma of coffee and bacon filled the room. Soon to be filled by cowboys, I enjoyed my breakfast and coffee in silence. Jane brought me a refill. In the background you could hear some of the other early risers talking the usual gossip.

Jane came and sat with me when she wasn't busy.

After my third cup of coffee I excused myself to go visit the Sheriff. He hadn't come in for breakfast and this had me a bit curious. As I entered the office, Pat was at his desk with a mug of coffee and George sitting off to the side with his own mug. They were in some heavy conversation which ceased immediately upon my presence.

"Is everything ok?" I asked taking a quick look around.

"Just a little jumpy I guess. Gonna be 30 or so cowboys in town some time early evening. We had no trouble with the last bunch. We can't be lucky every time we're visited by so many men at one time," he answered.

George sat there staring off in space. This had me worried for the Sheriff's sake. His side kick just didn't seem to be the pick to have at your side in time of trouble. He would be all right with gathering drunks or petty thieves but not much in a confrontation with gunplay.

Strange," Pat stated, "When they get to a town of any size, they can easily become jumpy and mischievous. That's when it's time to worry."

"Why worry. Cross that bridge when you get to it," I responded.

"Easy for you to say, you're not wearing the star," he retorted.

"Haven't seen anyone fitting the description Samuel gave, huh?" I asked with hope.

"No sir, sorry to say, Vince," he confessed.

"I'll catch you two later," answering as I walked out.

Outside on the walk was a sitting bench. It was a cool clear morning so I rolled a cigarette and decided to sit for a spell and watch the town wake to yet another cold day.

The general store was now open for business with customers entering and exiting carrying their goods: others are carrying boxes of supplies.

I watched Junior pull the blinds of his barber shop getting ready for his first customer. Figuring I could use a trim and shave, I figured this was as good a time as ever to get one. Junior had moved out West from New York to find his fortune in gold. He cut hair on site for extra money while mining his claim. He was almost killed in a mining accident so decided to move to town where he felt safer and opened his own barber shop.

"Looks like I'm in for a slow morning," glancing at the empty bench along the wall, "Cut your hair and I'll give you a free shave," he offered. "Be worth having someone around to talk to."

"Can't refuse an offer like that, especially when I need both," I said cordially, running my fingers under my chin, feeling the few days of growth.

"Everyone calls me Junior, mister," he said as he motioned me to have a seat.

"OK, then, Junior," I answered with a smile.

When he was finished, I got up and placed four bits in his hand, which covered the cost of the shave even though it was offered for free. By now there were two other gentlemen walking in, I nodded to them as I walked past.

"Have a good day Junior," I said, closing the door behind me.

The town was beginning to come alive, many being the cowboys who were expected today. Junior's business would be picking up today as I saw a sign on the wall offering baths also. I don't think he was getting rich with his barber shop, but he was a happy man with the gift of gab which the town's people liked.

Spotting a bench off to the right of me, I decided to again sit a spell and just watch the people.

Just as I sat I heard a crash of a wheel coming off a wagon. I looked up to see the terror in the eyes of a pretty young lady. She was pulling the reins back to stop the horse. Along side her was a cute little girl, must have been her daughter, both having scared looks on their faces.

I began to rise to see what I could do but was beaten by three other gentlemen more than willing to offer their services. I sat back down and watched them go to work helping this damsel in distress. I thought to myself what a friendly town.

The street had some pretty deep ruts which were now frozen. It was logical that the wheel caught up in one of them snapping the pin which held it to the axle. I didn't see any other damage and the gentleman had her on her way in just maybe 20 minutes or so.

It amused me to watch their actions as they walked away. Not hearing any comments, I listened to laughter and the slapping of hats on each other. I imagined the stories that would be told later this evening over a beer or two at the saloon.

The bank was now opening its doors with a line of minors and townsmen filing in to take care of business.

The bank was owned by Fred Williams also from New York. Being the only banker, he was well like and trusted. The bank guard was Roy Allen, an old gunfighter from back East whose past profession was not known by the town.

Fred hired Roy when he stopped a bank robbery just by being there coincidently.

Story has it that two men walked into the bank with intentions to rob it. As they walked in with masks on, they right away saw Roy and thought he was there to rob it. Knowing they were no match for Roy, they turned and high tailed it right out of town. The funny thing was Roy was in the bank at that time to repay a $300 loan back to the bank.

Fred was so relieved he hired Roy for the position of bank guard. Roy was getting up in years and had survived three gunshot wounds from the past and decided he would take the job and still be able to play his poker in the evenings.

Roy thought he might be fired if Fred ever found out his past, but the issue never came up.

There were two tellers who had been with Fred since the bank opened. Those who worked in the bank had much respect for each other. This made for a good work place. Nobody really knew how much Fred kept in the bank or even the reserve amount. Depending on the gold exchange office, it would often be quite a bit. Fred spared no expense when he purchased the safe. Without knowledge of safe fabrication or dynamite it was only Fred who had the combination. It was rumored that one other person could open the safe in case something happened to Fred, but no one in town knew who that person was. It could have been some one in the next town as far as anyone knew.

It was just before lunch when I noticed two rugged looking men riding up to the front of the bank on their horses. The taller of the two dismounted and went into the bank. Seconds later the second fella got down and flipped the reins of his horse one time over the rail. Most riders would flip the reins at least twice unless they were looking to leave in a hurry. Grabbing his saddle bags he also entered the bank. The way he carried them raised my suspicion. There was no effort in pulling them down off across the back of the horse leading me to believe that the bags were empty. Had there been anything in them, he would have carried them with his arm hanging: his arm was bent showing no effort from the lack of contents.

I made a quick glance over to the Sheriff's office but saw no horses.

There was something wrong. These two hombres didn't look like miners or businessmen. If they were ramrods from the nearby cattle run, they would be bringing money into the bank so that eliminated that theory too.

I didn't need trouble or to make a fool of myself on a mistaken hunch, but I had a bad feeling something was about to go down.

I got up and shifted my gun in the holster to make it easy to retrieve in case of trouble. The streets had thinned out some. It was pretty cold. The sky was painted a light blue with a few clouds gathering making the sun strain to get some warmth through. A dog ran out of the alley right in front of me startling me.

The bank was on my side of the street so I couldn't notice if the blinds had been pulled til I was almost in front of it.

Now I knew something was bad wrong.

I hesitated and gave a quick shuffle of my gun once more. I then walked over to the men's horses and flipped the reins a few more times. I stood off to the side as I didn't want to start any gunplay in the bank.

Just seconds later the bank door flew open and two shots thundered simultaneously. One of the men ran to his horse throwing the saddlebags over his horse. The second man came into view carrying no gun. His hand was bleeding quite badly.

The surprise came when they pulled on their reins and they didn't release.

The one robber looked up seeing me there. Looking down the barrel of a .45, he turned pale.

"Drop the gun," I yelled, "or die!"

I never witnessed what happened next. After making the motion of dropping the gun, he flipped it in a way I'd never seen before. I next heard the thunder from his gun. I had dropped my guard and now was feeling a shot enter my shoulder spinning me around and dropping me to the ground. Instinct as it was, I got a shot off. The bullet tore up his forearm which held his gun tearing a path and exiting at his elbow.

"Stay put or I'll send you to your maker!" I yelled in pain.

"They're not going anywhere," came a voice from the door of the bank.

I glanced over to see Roy holding his gun on both men. Bleeding pretty badly from his thigh, I recognized he had taken one but not without planting one of his own. The other robber was standing there with no gun in his now mutilated hand.

"There hasn't been a hanging in town for almost a year," he snapped, "so these two should set a good example."

"Where's the sheriff when you need him?" I asked.

"Does it look like we need a sheriff?" he snarled, holding his hip now, trying to stop the pain, "We can lock these two up ourselves and they can see the doc as soon as he's patched us up."

Four men came over and took the two gunmen to the jail house.

"Somebody get the doc for Roy and our friend here," someone yelled for the two outlaws to hear. "He'll tend to these two before looking at the others."

Fred came through the door with his shotgun ready, "They don't need no stinkin' trial," he yelled, "I'll core them right here and now."

Roy immediately put his hand on the shotgun pushing it toward the ground.

"If that goes off partner, you'll kill more than them. Let's let the law handle this. They'll get what's coming to them."

I looked at my shoulder. It looked pretty bad by the amount of blood I was losing. I must have been in shock because all I felt was a burning sensation.

As the doc arrived, I was standing next to Roy. He was looked pretty pale. Knowing he needed medical attention before me, I asked him to check out Roy first reassuring him I would live.

"Get Roy to my office before he drops," Doc ordered, "He's lost too much blood already. You come along too giving me a quick look over. Looks like a clean shot. I'll have you patched up in no time. Roy doesn't look so lucky."

Once we got to the Doc's office, he went right to work on Roy immediately pouring some type of new antiseptic over the hole scrubbing at the same time. Roy started to let out the yell of a lion but caught himself biting down on his lower lip instead.

Still in shock I only felt the burning of the antiseptic. He placed a clean cloth over the front hole then went to work to patch the bullet exit.

"You're a lucky man," he said as he wrapped my shoulder.

Jenny, the Doc's daughter, had Roy down on a table still wiping and cleaning his wound.

"Get him ready Jen. Get some whiskey down him," shouted the order, "We need to get that bullet out quickly: he's lost a lot of blood."

"I'm gonna run over to the Sheriff's office and check on those other two. I can wrap them to slow the bleeding, after that they can wait their turn."

The door shut with a bang and he was gone.

"Jan, what do you think?" Roy asked in a whisper, getting weaker.

"Don't rightly know, but I do know one thing. When a bullet goes in and don't come out, it means it hit something to make it stop, and that isn't good," she said with concern, "Drink some more whiskey, my dad will have you fixed up in a jiffy, don't you worry none."

The door opened with Fred filling the opening.

"I came as soon as I could Roy, had to lock up. The others were too nervous so I sent them home. How you two doin? How bout your friend?" speaking as he turned to look at my bandages.

"I'm gonna be fine, Roy's pretty hurt," I answered.

"He'll be fine when my Dad gets through with him," Jen answered, "He did some walking on that leg coming in, that's a good sign."

A short time later, the doc walked back in. "Got him ready, Jen?" speaking as he laid out his instruments next to Roy, "Get some hot water and lots of rags. The rest of you stay. I'll need him held tight so as I can retrieve that bullet without him squirming all over the place."

"Thank God that whisky about knocked him out," Doc whispered.

"What about those other two, Doc?" I asked.

"You bout shot that man's arm off," he said, "Wish you had cause now I get the privilege of cutting it off when I'm done with you two. The other won't be playing the pianny not without a finger. But where they're goin, I don't think it matters anyway." He went to work with his masterful hands removing the bullet.

"Looks more like muscle damage than bone," he said, as he let the bullet plunk into the tray next to the bed.

Jane came through the door carefully hugging me knowing the bandages were holding something together.

"I couldn't get here any faster and when I did Doc wouldn't let me in until he had you checked out," she complained.

Looking over at Roy she asked with concern, "How's Roy? He's going be all right isn't he?"

"Doc seems to think so, that's good enough for me," I answered in confidence.

The sheriff and George walked in giving an account for their absence.

"We just got back arresting three rustlers working down south some," the Sheriff stated, "They thought they'd help themselves to these cattlemen's live stock. Looks like a hanging of five after the jury gives their verdict."

I walked Jane out to the boardwalk. She wouldn't let go of my arm.

"Let's get you to your room and get you comfortable," she offered.

"No," I said like a spoiled kid, "let's just sit outside, I can use the fresh air. If I lie down now, I'd be out for days."

"I'm going to be right next to you as long as it takes you to get better," she promised.

"Any word on Scarface?" I asked.

"I'm sorry Vince, nobody with a scared face, not noticeable anyway. Jamie is on the lookout as well."

This was the first bullet I'd experienced. I hoped the last. The throbbing was now starting to bother me a lot as the shock was wearing off. I expected it to get worse as the night wore on and stay with me for a few days.

The moonlight was reflecting off Jane making her more beautiful than she already was. I could have admired her beauty for hours. I knew then I wanted her for my wife.

"Jane, will you marry me?" I blurted out.

"Oh yes, yes of course I will," she almost screamed, "Right away?"

"Yes honey, right away." I replied.

"I'll see the Sheriff in the morning and if you can talk Jamie to witness her sister marry the man who loves her, we'll do so as soon as your both ready. I know this is fast honey, but I'd like to be married before we leave town. It would only make it right," I stated. "There are a few things I should tell you first honey."

99

She cut me off walking up to me and putting two fingers on my like to stop my speech.

"I don't care of anything from the past, I love you and want you," she said with a quiet understanding tone. "I wish Jeb could have fallin for Jamie, all four of us could be riding out for a new life."

"I can only answer for us, honey," I surrendered. "Now go see Jamie."

It was seven o'clock when we left the Sheriff's office as husband and wife.

Chapter 15

I didn't think it was the right time to bring a few things up. I still had to find the man I was hunting for and I would never consider living in a town like Whitewater. All this would be brought up soon. I was almost sure it wouldn't matter to Jane. I felt she was ready to leave this town as much as I.

We spent the next hour watching the end of another day, but now Mr. and Mrs. Vince Masters.

The sky was clear and the air was cold. Jane was sitting so close to me I never felt the pain. Sometimes a person wishes time could stand still. This was one of those times.

The next morning brought us some disappointment. It was raining. My shoulder was throbbing more than yesterday. I knew I tossed all night upsetting Jane's sleep, but she never complained.

Jane went to the restaurant, I stayed in bed. As long as I didn't move my shoulder felt fine. Flat on my back was my most comfortable position so it was that way I remained.

While staring at the ceiling I noticed a fly just shy of the middle. If I was able I would have grabbed a swatter and smashed him. I laid there with a half smile on my face guessing I could get him with one shot with my .45. I think that darn fly knew my condition as he strutted back and forth to aggravate me.

After about a half hour of his teasing, I fell back to sleep for two more hours without even knowing it. The more sleep I got the better I felt when I woke.

I rested there for three days without leaving the bed except for the necessities. Jane was so good to me. She brought me meals and books to read in between my sleeping. She had gotten some type of herb from some Indian gal. The herb mixed with a small amount of whiskey gave me a complete solid sleep. With the weird dreams and the groggy state it left me in, I swore I would never touch that herb ever again after I recovered.

Each day I exercised my arm and shoulder beyond the point of severe pain. Wanting to get back to normal, I pushed myself ignoring the pain it was injecting. I had a job to do and I wanted to get back to my task as soon as possible.

One evening while Jane was out I was waking from sleep. Maybe it was a dream or a noise I just imagined. The noise came again, and now I was totally awake. It was clear the door knob was being jimmied.

It was very dark in the room. I fought to adjust my eyes the best I could to see clearer and grabbed my gun.

I slid down off to the side of the bed away from the door leaving two pillows end to end the long way. I pulled the covers up to give the illusion someone was still in bed. Then I waited.

If it were Jane, she would have used her key. If it were a friend, they sure would have knocked and addressed themselves. Someone was trying to get in without me being aware. The seconds seem like minutes. The door finally started to creek its way open. I figured it must have creaked too loudly for suddenly it stopped and I heard footsteps fade away down the hall. The intruder knew he had been discovered.

I was way too cautious to get up and look so I just laid still for a while to see what would happen. All of a sudden whoever it was returned thinking he hadn't wakened me since no light went on and the door was still cracked.

The door flew open exposing the shadow of a big man. Two shots bellowed out hitting the two pillows I had left covered. My plan worked. The third shot came from my gun blowing a hole dead center in his core.

When he dropped down on his side into a fetal position, I knew he was done for. I stood and walked over kicking his gun away from his reach.

He was holding on; by the look on his face, I knew it wouldn't be for long.

"Who are you mister?" I yelled, "Why did you try to kill me? Who hired you?"

"For the money," spitting blood with his words.

"Who? Who paid you? Give me a name!" I shouted.

"Half now the other half when I delivered your gun," he strained out.

"Who? Who?" I kept shouting, trying to keep him conscious enough to get a name.

"He'll be gone now, he said he would be leaving town, and he knows by now I failed."

"Who? Who? I kept yelling.

His final breath exhaled, another assailant dead. Another one not living long enough to give me a name.

Two men, the Sheriff, and Jane were at the door within minutes.

The hall was buzzing with speculation. My ears straining for some information I could use. But as my luck would have it, there was nothing.

"Anybody know this man?" the Sheriff asked.

"Think he came in with the cowboys, he's definitely new in town," said one of the men, looking down at him.

"OK, get him outta here. This is becoming a bad habit," the Sheriff complained.

"He told me before he died that he was hired to kill me. He said the fella that hired him would be leaving town if he failed. He never gave me the name before he died," I volunteered.

"I'm outta here as soon as we can get packed and our horses saddled. I may have a fresh trail to follow," I responded.

The Sheriff knelt down cleaning out the man's pockets hoping for some identification. There was none except some money and a paper with my room number on it. "Not much here, maybe enough to pay for damages. If he was paid in advance for your head, I'd like to know where it is," he muttered as he stood.

After everyone left I finally fell asleep but not before thinking of Jane. I loved her at my side always. I had no idea of where I was going or of what whether I was going to encounter to get there. We had been lucky up till now. This was going to be much too dangerous now. Morning came just way too soon. I could have slept for a few more hours, but I slid out of bed without disturbing Jane and went down for coffee and a quick breakfast. The Sheriff was already on his second cup as I entered the room. We talked some of my plans, and then I ate in silence. As I finished my coffee, I saw the Sheriff look around. Not being too surprised to what or who he was looking at.

Jane stood there watching and listening. "Are you sure you're able to travel Vince?" she finally asked.

"Don't worry about me honey, with you I'm as healthy as a horse," knowing my words were not fooling her.

She was gone in a flash. I knew she was going off to pack knowing somehow she would be ready to leave with out wasting a whole lot of time.

The next time I saw her she was dressed to kill; tight jeans, blouse, and jacket. This was one beautiful woman. As I eyed her, I couldn't help see she was wearing a pistol partially hidden under her coat.

"Don't worry Vince I can use it too," she responded before I even had a chance to question it.

I had no reason to doubt her, thinking maybe there are some things I don't totally know about her. All I wanted now was to get out of town. I'd look forward to a demonstration when we got out of town. This should be interesting.

"We'll leave in the morning honey. We need supplies, a pack mule, and a horse we can rely on," I said quietly.

"Taken care of," was her response. "I bought Kid Stevens horse, saddle, and gear, and I hired the stable boy to get supplies and pack mule."

That was one good horse. How she managed to acquire it was none of my business, so I didn't even ask. Thinking how beautiful she was, her smile and flirty ways probably got her quite a deal.

"What about your job at the restaurant?" I asked.

"My place is to be with you now. I'll show you I can be more than a wife."

I already found a friend to take my place. Richard wasn't happy when I told him I was leaving, but my friend Carol will do just fine for him."

I didn't sleep a wink that night. I loved Jane and wanted her at my side from now on.

What was I doing? I had no idea where I was going and less yet how to get there. The weather was showing some promise for traveling. That was a good thought as I knew the weather could change deadly at any given moment. It was bad enough I was putting myself in such danger and uncertainty, but how could I put Jane in that same scenario. It was her choice and I was glad she made it on her own. I remembered Jeb saying head north 40 miles then head west when we got to a fork in the road. He must have known something. There was sure to be a trail or some sign to where we would head west to take us through the mountains. If only I had a guide or someone else to travel with that knew the territory.

Jane had convinced me she was tough enough for the trip so she would now be my travel partner as well as a wife and I would have to rely on my own instincts to keep us both safe. If the weather should break to the worst or if we ran into a war party, we would both be in real trouble.

Then I thought of Scarface. Maybe with some real luck we would catch up to him frozen to death or in pieces missing his scalp. To me this could be the best thing to happen to him but it wouldn't give me the reason for all the killing. Though it would give me reason to go on with my life as I had no idea if I was really going to catch this hombre.

When this was over did I really want to go back home or make a life here in the West? Living at the ranch where my whole family had been murdered didn't appeal to me.

I had never been west, heck, I had never been any where. From how Jeb described the West, it was a paradise where a man could start a new life, where a man could live with a wife and raise little ones. I was sure these were decisions that could be decided at a later time.

As Jane and I woke up we knew this was to be the beginning of new adventures. When we finished breakfast, Jane went to the room to pack the necessities. I went for the pack mule. Looking at the sky I knew we needed to get started as soon as possible. Once at the livery stable I changed my mind and elected for a wagon with two mules. Intuition I guess as I thought about it through the night knowing bad weather could be a factor on this trip. The wagon could serve as many things in unknown territory. After all, it was safety for Jane I wanted so having a wagon would serve as shelter for the weather elements, a barrier from an Indian attack, as well as extra space for more supplies. At the end of the journey we could sell the wagon, mules, and the extra supplies.

When I pulled up to the hotel I could see a sigh of relief in Jane's eyes.

I pulled the tarpon back to fit the baggage and supplies. Then I refitted and adjusted the load securing it with a rope.

"The horses and mules are watered and fed, we're ready to go sweetheart," I announced.

I saw tears of happiness in her eyes as I helped her aboard now knowing what a disappointment it would have been to deny her this trip.

I left plenty of rein for the horses to the back of the wagon and gave the mules some slack once under way.

I had water and a rifle with plenty of ammo under the seat. I laid a blanket across the seat to comfort Jane.

We must have covered 30 miles that first day. Jane and I were still learning about each other as we talked all 30 miles. "This is so wonderful," she confessed, "I never would have imagined I would be heading west with such a great man, Vince. I love you so very much."

Her smile showed she was speaking straight from her heart. She had really softened me up inside where I had become so hard from the happenings from my past. Where we were heading was no place for a softy or to let one's guard down not if we were to survive.

The traveling was surprisingly comfortable. The trail we were on seemed to have been used often.

Rabbits seemed plentiful along the trail and finding fresh meat would surely be a pleasure on our first night at a campsite.

We traveled the last few miles after sunset with the moon already full giving us the light to set up camp. I saw a break along some heavy brush line and drove back into it giving us some security. Once we found a small opening, I stopped to set up camp.

It was still light enough to see Jane grab the Winchester and head off into the brush. It was just moments later I heard a shot. Two shots followed, and as I found out later she had gotten the second rabbit on the run.

She walked back into camp and threw three rabbits down in front of me. With a smile on her face she giggled, "I could have shot four but why kill more than we can eat. Do you want any more proof cause I can shoot a pistol just as good."

"Where did you learn all this?" I asked.

"I have three brothers," teasing me as she picked them up and started skinning.

I had no doubt in believing what I had just witnessed. She would be as good as any to watch my back. I just hoped we both had the instincts to survive any bad weather we should encounter.

After she skinned the rabbits, we both set out to collect kindling for a fire. In no time we had enough wood for dinner and to keep a small fire going till morning. I helped prepare the rabbits and put the coffee on. I left her to wander out to collect berries we had discovered while we were collecting the wood.

Food prepared on a campfire just can't be beat. We ate till we could eat no more. Then we kicked back and enjoyed the sounds of the wilderness. There was utter silence except for the crickets and the conversations between some ol' hoot owls.

After a while we unfolded the tarp and made sleeping room in the wagon. Rearranging the supplies we had just enough room to lay blankets. The sides helped protect us from the cold wind that was starting to blow as we were both uneasy with the thought of sleeping on the cold ground. The feeling of some protection in the wagon made us more comfortable.

The blankets were so intricately laid out by Jane with body warmth exclusively in mind. As we readied ourselves for sleep, I added wood to the fire one last time knowing it would last through the night. In the morning we should wake up to that nice warm glow to start a fire easily for breakfast and coffee.

I wanted to express how well our first day went but dared not to jinx ourselves. I climbed into the wagon and snuggled as close to Jane to combine our body heat for a good night's sleep.

Morning came fast. Waking up so close to Jane was another one of those moments any couple in love would wish to last forever. We must have both slept soundly as we woke up fresh and ready for breakfast. I needed to get up and get going. I knew the distance we would need to cover each day, but I chose to watch Jane stretch and move about thinking how beautiful she was and how lucky I was. She seemed so content, and that made me feel good inside. She looked so innocent climbing out from the covers that I noticed a little drool at the corner of her left lip. Such a lucky man was I.

I found myself thinking that this was the innocent lady that I was to spend the rest of my life with. After watching her with my rifle last night and the comments she made of the pistol, I guess there was more to this lady than I actually thought. I was sure I loved her even more now if that was possible.

I took a stick and stirred it in the orange flames until I started a small flame. I added some twigs to get it hot enough to ignite the larger pieces getting a fire started to cook our breakfast. Jane was right there moving along getting a few slabs of bacon, cracking eggs, and setting a couple of biscuits on a rock up close to the fire. We ate in silence as I stared off into the distance checking out the mountain range we were about to cross. One would wonder how a passageway through such a massive natural barrier would be possible. The clouds seemed to be building from all sides beginning to concern me.

We finished breakfast and packed the wagon. I started to wish Scarface was out there somewhere suffering in the mountains with a broken leg from a fall or dying of thirst or hunger. Maybe his horse would go lame enough to slow him down for me to catch up to him and serve the justice I had in mind for him. He had to know I was hot on his trail so I would have to be ready for a possible dry gulch while crossing over. Or would he wait and try again to hire a gun to try and stop me.

As we were ready to go, I checked once more making sure the campfire was out kicking a bit more dirt to fully cover it. Jane sat there in silence watching me with anticipation to get on our way. I jumped up and took the reins, snapped them lightly, and the mules had us on our way. Colt and Black Star (the name which Jane had given to Kidd Stevens' horse) started a comfortable pace. Colt did his usual ritual of bucking and kicking up his way of showing his normal attitude.

We were on the trail for the better part of the morning when I started to get the feeling we were getting close to where we would make a left to stay on course. I stopped the wagon and reached back grabbing the map from my saddlebags. This was the map that Jeb had given me and I was determined to follow it exactly as he had laid it out for me. Jane took the map and studied it for a few minutes.

"My guess would be we had a few more miles to go before we'd see any landmarks showing us were to turn," she said as she folded the map, "Hopefully there will be other wagon marks veering to the West also. I'd hate to miss the turn off, honey, we could end up in Canada or the North Pole." She sat in silence for a few moments. I thought she was checking out the area until she blurted out, "Honey, what are you gonna do if you can't find this man?"

I wasn't ready for a question like that but knew I had no plans of ever stopping until I did. Thinking real fast I answered, "I don't really know honey, let's get over these mountains and to the next town and we'll worry about that then." I hoped this was a good enough answer. She seemed to be satisfied checking out the area and starting small talk on different subjects. I thought good girl.

We must have made some good time keeping ourselves occupied in conversation or thought. All of a sudden Jane yelled out, "Look Vince, there's the trail we've been looking for, just ahead!"

As we approached, I was relieved to see the trail forked off. A closer look showed other horse prints and wagons that had headed west recently also. Since I wasn't a tracker, I had a hard time distinguishing horse tracks separately from horse tracks pulling wagons. I figured horses pulling wagons would leave deeper hoof marks.

How long ago were the tracks made? I got down and studied them as closely as I could. I saw some tracks had been filled with dust from the winds so the ones with the least amount of dust must be the freshest. I did notice a set of prints which hardly had any dust. My heart started beating. How I hoped I was on the right trail.

I wanted to pick up the pace with hopes of gaining ground on whoever we were following. If I ran the mules too hard I was scared I'd wear them out so I decided to just keep a steady pace and hope for the best.

The clouds were now closing fast and the temperature was dropping like a rock.

This had me worried. The higher up into the mountains we traveled, the more danger we would be in if the weather worsened. I knew inside I wanted to keep going but my instincts told me to find a small campsite for the night and continue in the morning. We traveled five more miles before finding a safe cul-de-sac protected by plenty of bushes to help barrier the cold winds.

After we made camp, I strolled over and checked out the wagon thoroughly. It seemed to be in good shape. The pin in the front axle pivot seemed loose, but I had no way of tightening it. I thought it would be all right as long as the conditions didn't worsen so I made a mental note of it and would check it periodically.

Colt and Black Star seemed to be restless and wanted to be untied. I filled two oat sacks and fed each. It was plain to see they welcomed it. I then untied the mules and tied them with plenty of slack to get to the grass. Jane and I saddled the horses and rode them on ahead to see what we were in for tomorrow. As usual, Colt bucked some but then settled down.

We rode on ahead a few miles to see what the terrain was going to be ahead. We decided things looked promising so we turned back. It was a nice ride even though cold and the horses needed to be ridden.

As we turned into the camp, a blur to my right shocked me as I recognized the blur of a mountain lion ready to pounce on my best mule. My pistol was out and fired two shots knocking it down. I knew the pistol would only wound and make a cat this size furious, so as he rolled trying to gain his balance, I grabbed my rifle and fired the fatal shot. The mules were in a full panic but settled down immediately.

"Nice shooting honey," Jane said in excitement.

"Thank God because this would not be the place to lose a mule," I answered with a cocky smile.

Night closed in fast. We forgot how cold it was as our adrenaline was high. The wind was picking up now and the temperature was on a fast drop. I knew this would be trouble if the weather stayed this way and I was right. As we woke, the snow was starting to fall.

We had a quick breakfast, loaded the supplies, and hit the trail. The clouds were dark and overlapping dropping snow harder and heavier. I wanted to get as far as we could and hoped to peak the mountain before the trail became impassable.

The mules took up the slack pulling the wagon at a steady pace. Colt and Black Star were comfortable with plenty of slack. Jane was bundled with extra blankets and looked quite comfortable showing confidence in my ability to handle the wagon.

The trail began a steep vertical climb tapering off in just a short distance. I kept slapping the reins to make some distance as the weather worsened. We turned following a blind bend finding the passage vanishing. It began to look as if the trail would be too narrow for the wagon. I showed no panic as to not worry Jane. I stopped the team and did a complete check of the condition of the wagon and harness.

When I was sure everything was safe, I walked to the front of the mules. I would lead them through the narrow section making sure the wagon didn't drag against the bank or hit any fallen rocks.

It seemed like miles as the traveling slowed. Rolling quite a few rocks over the side listening to them crash down the side of the mountain even made me more cautious. The snow suddenly came down so heavy it slowed visibility to a mere minimum. When the trail opened, it came with a sigh of relief. Not wanting to stop, I jumped back on the wagon and reined the mules setting a quicker pace. It wasn't long before we reached the mountain.

The team followed the trail as if they traveled it daily. Jane noticed my eyes fading from lack of sleep and relieved me of the reins. The snow was still falling hard showing no mercy for our safety.

All of a sudden I saw the faint outline of a man. At first I thought I was seeing things as tired as I was but as we got closer, a tall brawny fellow with a low slung gun hanging at his side came clearer into view. As we came up to him, he was clear as day. The scar on his face magnified in my brain telling me I had been caught off guard. I went for my gun but his was already drawn and before I cleared leather, I felt a sharp pain in my side and then the roar of a gun. All I remembered was hearing a click from my gun. As I fell back into the wagon I still was alert enough to know my gun had misfired. I shook my head to clear it and found myself looking into the face of the man I was supposed to kill. He stood there looking at me letting out a roar of laughter as he lifted his gun to finish me off. At that instant I woke with a yell, soaking in sweat from head to toe.

Jane was yelling, "Vince, Vince, wake up! Wake up!"

"Bad dream," I answered.

She pulled back on the reins to stop the mules, then gave me a hand back up into the seat.

"You scared the heck out of me, Vince. First you were there and then you weren't," she said shivering.

It was then I realized the shock of terror on her face and my feeling a terrible pain in my side at the same time. I looked down to see blood staining through my coat. Pulling my coat open I revealed I had indeed been shot. On further examination, we saw it was a clean shot that had entered and exited without much damage. That didn't ease the pain. Jane grabbed a shirt and wiped the wound then wrapping and tying it off to slow the bleeding. Squinting I scanned the area the best I could. The snow was still falling quite heavily so visibility was only a few feet.

"He must have known it was a blind shot. Thinking he missed, he must have retreated. If he thought he had hit me, he would have run up and finished the job." I explained to Jane. "As long as the snow keeps falling this heavy, we should be safe. He knows we'll be alert now."

I hoped that he was thinking that way. We were going to have to stop sometime soon to have a better look at the wound and care for it accordingly. One thing was sure. We were on the right track and the enemy was not far ahead of us. The wound was to my left side so it wouldn't hinder my shooting ability if it was needed. I hoped it was Scarface and not another hired gun. With luck I would catch up to this mystery man and finish what I'd started out to do.

It was beginning to make sense now why we would be attacked in this area. If he had been successful, he would have been able to send the wagon and bodies over the edge of the cliff leaving us undiscovered till spring.

The pain wasn't as bad as I expected. It must have been the cold numbing the wound keeping the pain to a minimum.

We continued as fast and safely as we could. I figured we should be heading to the last batch of mountains reaching the next town within the next two days. I was now thinking the worst scenarios the weather warming changing the snow to ice and really making the last of our travel treacherous.

We set up camp in an area hidden by short but thick pines. Here we would get some rest and tend to my wound.

I tended to the horses as best as I could with the pain. Jane fixed a quick meal before tending to my wound. The bullet luckily entered and exited less than an inch to my side making it a lot less dangerous but the pain was the same. We would have to sleep under the wagon this night to escape the amount of snow which was still falling. Jane went out to fetch some kindling for a fire. Within a hour we were huddled together close to the fire eating biscuits and gravy with hot coffee to warm our bodies. The pain in my side was bearable. When I woke it felt like I had been shot all over again. I got up and tended to the horses, helped pack the wagon and the pain seemed to lessen some.

The snow had slowed some bringing with it some visibility. Jane and I kept a close eye out for anything out of the ordinary. We crested the last major mountain so descending was a sigh of relief. Over the next few mountain tops we could see smoke rising into the sky which meant civilization. I figured we still had a day of travel before we got to the sight of the next town or settlement.

The rest of the trip was pretty much uneventful. We were finally seeing a break in the sky and the warm rays of sun did little for our cold bodies. We stopped to rest and water the horses one last time. I checked my fire arms and ammo. I sure didn't need a misfire from one of my guns dream or not. Evening was coming fast.

As we approached the outskirts of the town, we heard notes from an out-of-tune piano making its way to evening air. The last few flurries of snow were spotty refusing to give up totally. As the clouds broke open, you could see the moon fighting its way through the thinner cloud lines.

Jane looked at me with a warm smile knowing the worst was over. We survived what mother nature had tested us with.

"It's gonna be nice to sleep in a nice warm soft bed tonight honey," she said, "I hope we can find a doctor this late in the evening. I'd like to have him check that wound and bandage it correctly."

"It's gonna be all right sweetheart," I answered, "Let's just see if we can get a room, bath, and a warm meal for right now. I'm gonna need some sleep soon; we'll find the doctor in the morning. Keep alert for any stranger showing any interest in our presence."

Every shadow looked like a threat as we reined the team down to the livery. Many lanterns along the street were lit giving enough light to watch for danger.

People were still walking the sidewalks going about their business as if it were still early. None seemed to mind at all as we passed.

I didn't expect to see so many wagons as we approached the livery. There was a young man brushing a white Palomino who came over to greet us. He was about six feet tall, a solid build with long straight blonde hair.

"Can I be of help to you?" he asked anxiously.

Grabbing on to the bridle of the horse to keep it from advancing, I saw him give stare to my wounded side. Still staring, he was as stiff as a statute.

"Hey pal," I snapped, "Yes, I've been shot. We were ambushed back in the hills. Is there a doctor in this town?"

Coming back to reality he comprehended what I had just said as he gave a quick glance over to Jane then back at my shoulder.

"Yes sir," he finally answered, "Just down the street. You'll see his office marked. It's right next to the general store."

"Thanks," I returned, "If you could take care of the team and the two back there, I'd be most grateful." Flipping a two dollar gold piece to him I added, "Spoil them with oats afterwards."

"You bet mister, anything else?" he asked anxiously.

"Maybe," I returned, "You notice a man riding into town in the past hour or two? He'd be big, ugly and hiding a scar behind a fairly thick beard. Probably riding alone."

He stood there for a few moments thinking, 'Well, a fella came in with that description alright. Came in yesterday afternoon. Can't say for sure I saw any scars and not a bit pleasant either," he paused still thinking, "He looked pretty tired if you ask me like he'd been riding a while without any sleep."

My side started to hurt real bad with blood fighting its way through the bandages Jane had applied.

"Thanks for the information. I want the doctor to check this wound, then I want to come back and check out this man's horse," I announced.

"Can't help ya there. He didn't leave it," the kid answered, "He had me wipe him down and feed him. Came back about an hour later and fetched him. He the one that did that to ya mister?"

"The less you know, probably the better off you'll be," I answered.

Jane and I got down and walked over to the doctor's office which was no more than 50 yards from the livery. I knocked as we walked in. The place looked real clean, but no one came to greet us. All of a sudden a door opened and a man came through. After a short explanation of what had happened, he had me take a seat and went to work.

He removed the strips Jane had applied, and saw infection setting in.

"I'm going to have to clean this up. Right now it looks to be a surface infection which is pretty common. Had you let it go much longer, you may have been in trouble," he noted.

With a bowl of warm water and soap, he commenced the cleaning procedure, which meant scrubbing to the point of me wanting to pass out from pain.

"I'm sorry mister, but I have to do this," apologizing to me.

When he had the area cleaned, he applied some kind of ointment over the wound explaining it should prevent any more infection. Then he wrapped it with new bandages and warned me to take it easy giving it a chance to heal. Thanking him, I paid his fee and we were headed back out to the street.

Looking up and down the street, we saw two hotels close by.

"That one will do, honey," I said, pointing to the newer looking of the two.

We registered at the desk. I paid in advance and we were escorted to our room. Jane left for quite a while to return bathed and prettied up. She brought a pail and water to wash me up as best she could without getting the bandages wet. Shortly after we were both asleep.

I took the advice of the doctor and laid back resting for three days. Jane would go out and bring food serving me in bed.

The fourth day I was too restless to stay in another second. It was the afternoon so I thought I would go out for some fresh air. Jane was comfortable resting so I left without disturbing her.

Chapter 16

Once outside I wandered the streets finding myself coming up to the saloon. Once in front I decided to go in and look around, see what I could find out. Walking through the bat wings I could immediately saw poker was pretty popular in this town. More than half the tables were hosting four to five players at each. No one seemed to notice me as I walked in. I went straight to the bar and ordered a beer. Even the bar was crowded with men talking and laughing at stories each was telling. I found myself standing by myself without the first person showing any curiosity to whom I was or why I was there. Was this town that large that strangers weren't even noticed?

Looking around I saw an empty chair at one of the poker tables. It was probably vacated by some poor sole that had lost enough for one evening.

I strolled over and asked, "Mind if I sit in?" No one responded.

Finally one man to my left looked up from his cards and nodded his approval to sit. I took that as a yes and sat. Laying some bills on the table I asked, "Five card?"

"Yes sir, no limit," the man on the left answered.

Not much but small talk between these men. As I looked across the table from me was a man I swore I knew. Finding me staring at him, I was suddenly shocked to see signs of some pretty deep scars under his thick beard. Scars that definitely were made by finger nails.

"What are you staring at mister?" he asked in a real rough voice.

I couldn't deny I was subconsciously staring without even realizing it. My heart started to pound wanting to come right out my chest. I was caught dead to rights. Swallowing hard hoping no one noticed, "Nothing," I answered. I didn't want to admit he looked familiar afraid I would raise suspicion.

"Then play your hand or fold," he growled, "The bet's fifty to you."

I had been paying no attention to my cards since I was, interested in this fellow across from me. Three, threes and deuces, I threw in to stay in the game.

I took that hand and the next seven of twelve I played. Starting to have quite a stack of bills in front of me, I began seeing disappointment along with suspicion from the other players.

The next few hands when the pots were low I folded even if I had a winning hand. I wanted to find out more about this man sitting across from me. Even though I introduced myself when I sat down, only two others gave they're names.

I had to find out about this fellow. Who was he? Why did he look so familiar to me? I didn't need to jump to conclusions or do something foolish without knowing for sure.

I caught myself looking at him from time to time but stopped myself and immediately brought my attention back to my cards.

I also got the feeling he was doing the same as I caught him glancing at me more than the others.

Reaching down I loosened my gun in the holster just in case something was to happen between the two of us.

My next thought was to mention where I was from and see what response I would get from him. With hope he would react with nervousness or sweat.

Chapter 17

It was getting late and most of the other tables in the room were becoming vacant. If I was going to do this I had to do it now.

Swallowing hard I was about to execute my plan when a voice came from behind me. I never even heard anyone walk up one reason I always liked my back to the wall.

"You killed my friend Kid Stevens," the voice growled.

This I didn't need. My side still hurt to the point I wasn't sure I could draw to my full potential. I knew I could draw as fast with my left hand but unfortunately I wasn't wearing two guns at this particular time. This left me at somewhat of a disadvantage.

"You killed my friend, now I'm gonna kill you," he announced.

Thinking now this was all bad. I had the man I was suspicious of being the man I had been searching for sitting right in front of me. With a man who now wants to kill me to my back.

I looked to the man sitting in front of me finding him starring coldly at me. I had no choice. I didn't want to get it in the back. Many left the saloon as I was contemplating

123

my next move. Others cleared to the side of the room with anticipation of a gunfight. Obviously the sheriff was nowhere around, and the bartender was standing behind froze. I knew there was going to be a gunfight.

Cautiously and slowly I stood up, standing sideways so I could keep an eye on both men. My challenger was a young kid, clean cut, tall lanky fellow. His hand was down by his low-slung pistol.

I took a few steps back to clear the other men sitting at the table keeping them out of the line of fire.

"You're not gonna be so lucky this time as you were with Stevens," be barked.

"We drew on each other many a time, friendly like and I always out drew him." he bragged.

I thought to myself. Who was he trying to convince. I didn't think this kid was too sure of himself because he was talking too much.

"You sure you want to do this kid?" I asked.

"Don't call me kid!" he yelled.

"If you go for that gun kid, you're not gonna grow any older," I warned.

"You called me out," I answered in a low tone. "It's your move."

As he was bringing his gun up out of the holster, I heard my gun roar out and watched him take a step back from the force of the bullet.

Staring at me with a glaze already covering his eyes, he fell back to a sitting position still holding his gun. He wanted to say something but blood was pouring from his mouth making a gurgling sound. Falling to his back, I knew he'd be growing no older.

Adrenalin must have taken hold of my body as my shoulder was feeling no pain for those few seconds. Then I could feel it coming back, but it was bearable.

Then I realized I had taken my eye off the card player. Glancing over quickly I found the chair he was sitting in was now vacant. He was no where in sight.

No, this can't be, I thought to myself. The others were still seated with looks of amazement.

"Where did that man sitting there go?" I screamed at the others.

"Who was he?" asking again.

"He didn't give a name. Why are you asking about him?" one of the others asked. "He came and sat in just before you came, ordering to deal him in, he didn't leave a name."

Moments later the sheriff came in and a few of the men gave their account of what went down. My story was the same so he had no choice but to claim it self defense.

Looking down at the kid, "I recognize this one, there's quite a reward on him."

Looking up at me he said, "Come to the office in the morning and collect it. I suggest everyone go home now, it's late."

The card player had to be my man. I would not forget him. Why did he look so familiar to me? I came through many towns to get where I was now and saw a lot of faces. Could that be it?

I had to find him and confront him. He would have only one chance to convince me he was innocent. If he couldn't within a reasonable doubt, I would force him into a gunfight and kill him.

Why didn't I confront him sooner at the table when he asked me what I was looking at? That was my opportunity and I blew it. At least I knew the face I was after now. I had the feeling my search was over. It would end in this town. I would soon be free of this nightmare and get on with my life with Jane.

I grabbed my winnings, folded the paper money, and slipped it in my vest pocket.

Then an alarming thought came over me. Get to the stables as quickly as possible.

There were a few men still in the streets mumbling small talk paying me no attention as I went by. They were probably rambling on over the gunfight they had witnessed just moments ago.

As I got to the stables I found the card player mounting his horse for a quick get away. I knew this as I saw the cinch of the saddle was loose telling me he had hurried to get out of there.

"Freeze fella," I ordered, "You're not going anywhere. Now get down real slow, keep your hands where I can see them. Go for your gun and I'll kill ya before you clear leather. Don't go for your gun and I'm probably gonna kill you any way. Walk over here where I can see ya."

There were a few oil lamps on low flame giving off soft light. Moonlight was shinning through the double door giving some additional light.

"Keep your hands clear of that gun," I warned.

"Look mister, I don't know who you think I am, but let's talk," he begged, "You a law man?

"No," was all I could answer.

"I thought you were and that's why I ran," he explained, "I'm wanted by the law and I don't intend going back to jail."

"If you're who I think you are, you're not gonna have to worry about going to jail," I warned, "I intend to put you six feet under."

"Who are you? Why have you been following me, what do you want with me? he retorted.

"Shut your mouth," I ordered, "I'll be the one asking the questions."

He stood for a few seconds looking real pale and not knowing what to do.

"Unbuckle that gun belt real careful like and let it drop to the ground," I ordered.

"Ok, please don't kill me," he begged, "I'll do as you say."

Quivering like a coward he reached down and unbuckled the belt letting it drop. As it hit the ground I began to feel a sensation throughout my body. I never rationally thought through what I'd do when I got to this point. I always promised myself I was gonna kill him on sight. Now I knew it would be wrong.

Now he was unarmed. I couldn't shoot him now even if he confessed to everything. I was now forced to turn him over to the law for a fair trial.

"What are you gonna do now?" he asked with sweat pouring down his face.

"Nothing right now. You're gonna answer questions I ask, and the first lie I hear, I'm gonna kill ya." I promise, "What's your name?"

"You have to turn me in to the Sheriff," he retorted.

"I may just do that, but you can go healthy or with a bullet in your leg, shoulder, or arm maybe? Now answer me, what's your name!" I ordered, taking aim at his left thigh pulling the hammer back making sure he heard it.

"Ok, Ok," he responded, "my name………."

Then in a flash I saw his arm come around bringing a knife in one smooth movement. I was so alert to what he might do I fired sending the knife flying along with some flesh of his hand.

I had forgotten about the possibility of a knife till I remembered how Katie was so savagely killed.

"You are one stupid man," I retorted composing myself. "I should kill you for that, and have every right to. One more stunt like that and I will. Now you have five seconds to tell me your name or you're gonna be crawling to get to the sheriff's office."

"Charlie Lang, my name's Charlie Lang," he surrendered.

It was coming back to me now. I was very young, but now I remembered why he looked so familiar to me. He was related some how to Chester Lang.

"Chester's brother?" I asked.

"Yeah, Chester's my brother," he confessed.

Looking at him more closely now, I could see features of his brother that I remembered which were slight. I was just a young pup when Chester worked for my Dad. Even with all the years that had passed, I knew this man was telling the truth. Could he be a twin? The age looked right. If he told me it was so, I would also believe him.

"Why'd you do it? Why would you kill my whole family? Why Katie?" I asked.

"I need a doctor," looking down at his hand, "please, send for a doctor."

"You're gonna need an undertaker if you don't start talking," I responded, "Then maybe, just maybe, I'll get you to the doc."

He stood there holding his hand, blood dripping to the ground. He was looking at me with horror in his face. I could see he was trying to find the words to explain his actions. There was no doubt I had the right man. This was the man I tracked through three states. This was the man who hired professional gunman to try and stop me. This was the man who thought he could get away with such a hideous crime. Now this was the man who was going to meet his maker.

"Lang," I ordered, "So help me I'm gonna start putting bullets in you one by one until I have the whole story."

"I owed a lot of money from a gambling debt. I was given a short time to repay it or be killed. Chester had talked of the 3M Ranch often. I pried information from him little at a time to prevent any suspicion. I asked questions only when I knew he had been drinking and wouldn't remember me asking. He told me the wealth of your family and gave a perfect description of the ranch. My prying stopped whenever I saw him become suspicious. He told be of the members of the family and of how many cowhands were employed. I guess it slipped my mind when he told me there were two sons. I knew I would never get away with robbing the national bank. I thought robbing a ranch would be easier. Chester spoke of your father's desk and the money he kept there. He also told me of the safe that would be impossible to access so I decided to take a chance with the desk. Time was running out on my debt, I became desperate. That's when I decided to take the chance.

He stopped talking all of a sudden. I knew he was scared to confess to the assassination of my family, seeing how unstable I was, with a gun pointing at him. He was right. If he decided another desperate move as he did with the knife, I would have shot this coward right where he stood.

"Please he once more begged," I need a doctor."

"Keep talking," I ordered, "Why my whole family?"

I was in town when I ran into your sister. The description Chester gave was right on the money. When I heard someone yell to her to give regards to Robert and remind him of the next cattle meeting that following week, I knew I had the right girl. While she was in the livery I snuck over and loosened the pin on the rear wheel of her wagon.

Following her out of town a few miles, the pin finally dropped out. She stopped before the wheel fell off. I stayed back out of sight to see what she was going do. I watched her get down and look at the wheel. A short time after, I heard a horse approaching. I guess it was her brother as he called out her name.

Chapter 18

I rode up from behind and offered my assistance. Your brother refused saying he had it under control. I rode up next to them asking if they thought they were too good to have a trail rover help them; the lady swung a whip at me. I grabbed it pulling her to the ground.

Your brother went for his gun, but I got mine out first, plugging him twice.

Your sister was one frisky gal. I got down and grabbed her, that's when she dug her nails into my face. She was still in my arm struggling when she went to dig in. I pulled my knife and pressed it in her back, twice as I remember before she relaxed and slid to the ground. That was too bad, because I really wanted to get to know her better, right there, right in front of her dead brother.

I was furious. I wanted to kill him now without any more explanation. I might have except I turned hearing the Sheriff enter the stable.

Vince," he warned, "I heard everything. I was at the door listening while he confessed with what he did with your sister. I knew I better come in before you did something you'd regret. Frankly I wouldn't have blamed you if you had shot him. He can tell the rest of the story to the judge, and then the whole town can watch him hang. I'm sorry Vince."

"Watch you're back mister, this ain't over for you. That's a promise," George warned.

I knew what he meant, but right now I wasn't concerned about it. What Sam warned me about always stayed in the back of my mind. Everyone George had hired to kill me in the past failed. I felt invincible now and would be ready knowing I would prevail. I promised myself not to let Jane get any wind of what he just said.

Handcuffing him, the Sheriff spun him toward the door.

"I need a doctor," he kept begging.

The Sheriff showed him no mind, shoving him toward the door.

I was relieved when the Sheriff showed up because my finger was tightening on the trigger as George was telling of my sister. Had the gun gone off, I would have had no remorse.

I walked back toward the hotel where I found Jane looking for me.

"Is everything alright honey?" she asked with concern, "I've been looking all over for you. People are saying you shot someone."

Honey, the man I was hunting for is in jail and will hang. I will be there to look into his eyes as they drop him. In a few weeks this will all be over. I want to go West to meet up with Jeb. We will decide then what to do and where our destiny will take us.

There's a big world out West waiting for us, a ranch back in Arkansas. The only decision we have to make is where we want to raise a family.

"Oh Vince!" She replied.